A Dawn of Guardians

A Shade of Vampire, Book 33

Bella Forrest

Copyright © 2016 by Bella Forrest.
Cover design inspired by Sarah Hansen, Okay Creations LLC
Formatting by Polgarus Studio

All rights reserved.

No part of this book may be reproduced in any form or by any electronic or mechanical means, including information storage and retrieval systems, without written permission from the author, except for the use of brief quotations in a book review.

Also by Bella Forrest:

THE GENDER GAME
The Gender Game

A SHADE OF VAMPIRE SERIES:

Series 1:
Derek & Sofia's story:

A Shade of Vampire (Book 1)
A Shade of Blood (Book 2)
A Castle of Sand (Book 3)
A Shadow of Light (Book 4)
A Blaze of Sun (Book 5)
A Gate of Night (Book 6)
A Break of Day (Book 7)

Series 2:
Rose & Caleb's story:

A Shade of Novak (Book 8)
A Bond of Blood (Book 9)
A Spell of Time (Book 10)
A Chase of Prey (Book 11)
A Shade of Doubt (Book 12)
A Turn of Tides (Book 13)
A Dawn of Strength (Book 14)
A Fall of Secrets (Book 15)
An End of Night (Book 16)

Series 3:
Ben & River's story:

A Wind of Change (Book 17)
A Trail of Echoes (Book 18)
A Soldier of Shadows (Book 19)
A Hero of Realms (Book 20)
A Vial of Life (Book 21)
A Fork Of Paths (Book 22)
A Flight of Souls (Book 23)
A Bridge of Stars (Book 24)

Series 4:
A Clan of Novaks

A Clan of Novaks (Book 25)
A World of New (Book 26)
A Web of Lies (Book 27)
A Touch of Truth (Book 28)
An Hour of Need (Book 29)
A Game of Risk (Book 30)
A Twist of Fates (Book 31)
A Day of Glory (Book 32)

A SHADE OF DRAGON:

A Shade of Dragon 1
A Shade of Dragon 2
A Shade of Dragon 3

A SHADE OF KIEV TRILOGY:

A Shade of Kiev 1
A Shade of Kiev 2
A Shade of Kiev 3

BEAUTIFUL MONSTER DUOLOGY:

Beautiful Monster 1
Beautiful Monster 2

For an updated list of Bella's books,
please visit www.bellaforrest.net

Join my VIP email list and I'll personally send you an email reminder as soon as my next book is out!
Click here to sign up: www.forrestbooks.com

Contents

Prologue: Sofia 1
Chapter 1: Grace 17
Chapter 2: Hazel 25
Chapter 3: Hazel 31
Chapter 4: Hazel 47
Chapter 5: Hazel 53
Chapter 6: Hazel 69
Chapter 7: Hazel 91
Chapter 8: Hazel 107
Chapter 9: Hazel 129
Chapter 10: Hazel 167
Chapter 11: Hazel 179
Chapter 12: Hazel 191
Chapter 13: Hazel 201
Chapter 14: Hazel 217
Chapter 15: Hazel 229
Chapter 16: Ruby 239
Chapter 17: Hazel 247
Chapter 18: Hazel 253
Chapter 19: Hazel 257

Chapter 20: Hazel 265
Chapter 21: Hazel 293
Chapter 22: Ruby 299
Chapter 23: Rose 305

The "New Generation" Names List

- **Arwen:** (daughter of Corrine and Ibrahim - witch)
- **Benedict:** (son of Rose and Caleb - human)
- **Brock:** (son of Kiev and Mona – half warlock)
- **Grace:** (daughter of Ben and River – half fae and half human)
- **Hazel:** (daughter of Rose and Caleb – human)
- **Heath:** (son of Jeriad and Sylvia – half dragon and half human)
- **Ruby:** (daughter of Claudia and Yuri – human)
- **Victoria:** (daughter of Vivienne and Xavier – human)

Prologue: Sofia

A lot had happened in the last two years.

A *lot*.

On a personal note, Vivienne and Xavier had become grandparents to a beautiful human-werewolf hybrid. Vicky had experienced a few scares during the pregnancy but with the diligent help of Corrine, she'd managed to give birth to one of the cutest baby boys I'd ever laid eyes on. Jovi Blackhall was his name. (Bastien shunned his Mortclaw parents' name in favor of his surrogate parents', who'd always felt more like his true parents to him anyway.) With gray-blue eyes and curly black hair, Jovi would be five months old at the end of this month. He was showing no signs that he had the ability to morph, but he was hairier than a regular human baby, and he was definitely showing early signs of supernatural strength. His grip was as hard as a twelve-year-old's, and he had a full set of teeth (which caused Vicky a lot of grief during breastfeeding).

Lucas, for the first time in his over five hundred years of living, got hooked enough by a woman to tie the knot. Not only had he vowed to remain true to Marion forever, he'd also promised to be a father to her child, Avril (which, so far, he seemed to be doing a commendable job at). Their wedding had been held among the rocks at the base of the lighthouse. Derek, as Lucas' best man, had looked prouder than I'd ever seen him of his brother. Prouder than when Lucas had survived The Dewglades… Prouder than when Lucas had survived The Underworld. Yeah, committing himself to a woman was a big step for

Lucas. He was no longer a skittish bachelor. Derek had his fair share of fun with his older brother that day, including swiping Bella and Brett's naughtiest ogre toddler and wrapping him up as a wedding gift. And Marion had plans to become a vampire once Avril grew a bit older.

Lawrence had gotten down on one knee before Grace last Christmas, after our family dinner. Grace—bless her heart—had burst into tears before throwing herself into his arms and accepting his proposal. They'd married this year in the spring in an exquisite ceremony held in The Hearthlands, following in the path of her parents. I had cried like a baby on seeing Grace in her wedding dress. It had brought back the memory of River walking down the aisle toward my son. Grace had positively sparkled in her gem-encrusted white gown, fashioned by dragon seamstresses. Heath, who had moved permanently to The Hearthlands, presided over the ceremony and their vows, which was lovely to see. Grace and Lawrence had just recently left The Shade for their honeymoon in the Alps.

Another recent coupling was Arwen and Brock. They'd gotten engaged in the New Year—something that had caused Corrine and Kiev to have another one of their little, ahem, "heart-to-hearts".

Orlando and Maura, who'd remained with us in The Shade, had also caught the love bug—Orlando had been seen hanging out a lot with Regan, the half-human, half-dragon twenty-year-old daughter of dragon Azaiah. Orlando was a couple of years her senior, and from what I could gather, they were getting along like a house on fire… so to speak.

Azaiah wasn't too pleased about that, to say the least. Regan was a rare creature; she was one of the dragon hybrids on the island who was able to shift into a beastly form, in spite of her mixed blood. And a stunning beastly form at that. Azaiah wanted Regan to end up with a fire dragon—the fire dragons were still in great need of females to increase their population—but he wasn't going to interfere with his daughter's happiness, so he let the couple be. I supposed at the back of his mind he was hoping the relationship wouldn't last, and he'd be able to introduce her to a strapping Hearthlands native. Only time would tell whether he'd get his wish.

As for Orlando's sister, Maura, it had taken her about a month to make a full recovery from her former Bloodless state, and once she was out of the hospital and roaming around the island, River's halfblood-Hawk son, Field, had caught her eye. Neither Field nor the other four Hawk boys had shown a lot of interest in girls—in my opinion, they were shy of them. It had been Maura who'd initiated the friendship with Field and coaxed him out of his shell, and now they were dating.

Aisha had become the mother of a healthy baby girl, whom they'd called Riza. She and Horatio had been on cloud nine for weeks, wrapped up in their own little bubble. Riza was the first jinni baby most of the Shade residents had ever seen. Unlike her parents, her bottom half wasn't covered. Apparently it was jinn custom that children began to cover their lower halves at the age of six, when they were old enough to understand its significance.

Jinni babies could almost pass for humans, were it not for their thick jaws and inherent magical powers.

My father and Kailyn were still proud parents to their adopted werewolf son, whom they'd named Hunter. Saira, Micah and Kira were relishing their roles as parents to the other two cubs. We had asked the werewolves from The Woodlands whom we'd worked with over the years if anybody knew of the cubs' biological parents. Based on the cubs' pure white fur, the werewolves had an idea of whom they had belonged to—but informed us that the pack had gone missing some years ago. Perhaps the harpies had been responsible for that.

As for the gray babies, soon after TSL's victory over the IBSI, Shayla and I had made a special visit to The Sanctuary to speak to the Ageless and her sisters. We figured that if the sisters and their council didn't know what the babies were, who would? Well, the witches did claim to know. They said that the babies were incubi, demonic horned creatures who, once they grew old enough, stalked prey in the night and were known to do… unsavory things to them while they slept. Those gray babies were definitely *not* on the cards for staying in The Shade. We couldn't just abandon them, though. They had still been infants after all. We had no idea how the harpies had originally gotten hold of them, but the witches agreed to take them off our hands and attempt to return them to the land of the incubi (somewhere I would rather not approach within a thousand miles of).

That experience with the mysterious gray babies truly opened our eyes as to how little we had scratched the surface of the supernatural world. It both struck me with awe and made me feel small to think that we had probably still only come across a fraction of the species that lived in the parallel dimension.

Which leads to what else changed over the past two years. On a professional note… Well, where to even begin?

After our victory over the IBSI, we were formally announced as their replacement, so there was much, much work to be done in terms of structural organization. We had a huge fleet of people to train. We had to teach every member of our new organization, as well as every volunteering member of the public, how to administer the cure. Then we had the even greater task of disseminating the cure to such a large volume of Bloodless. We worked tirelessly, day in and day out for months, until finally we had quelled the worst of the virus. The rest was a matter of stamping it out wherever we happened across the odd victim. Although we could never become complacent, we had spread enough awareness about the cure and its administration to ensure that the virus would never become rampant again.

Lives were saved. Families were reunited. Members of TSL were declared heroes and held in much higher esteem as fighters and protectors of humankind than the IBSI had ever been. Over the months, we had been featured on the news so much we became like movie stars. We couldn't go anywhere these days without being recognized—at least, the core members of our group couldn't: Derek and I and our immediate family and closest friends, who were at the heart of TSL's leadership.

Three months after taking over from the IBSI, we decided to change TSL's name. The Shadow League no longer seemed like an appropriate name for our organization. We were no longer shadows. We were the predominant protective organization. Thus, we changed our name to the Global Agency for Supernatural Protection, aka GASP.

Derek was the formal chairman of GASP and was ultimately in charge of making decisions. He was the CEO, the boss man, whatever you wanted to call him. This was a role that my husband slotted into easily. As reluctant a king as he might've been in the earlier stages of his life, he was used to the role of leadership by now, and he bore the responsibility better than anyone. The rest of us had high management positions—and in those early months of suppressing the Bloodless, each of us had a specific region that we were responsible for.

But once the Bloodless were no longer a threat, the focus of GASP shifted to the second problem that had plagued Earth for decades—a problem that the IBSI had never been well-equipped to solve: the problem of meddlesome supernaturals other than Bloodless. Supernaturals who came from the supernatural dimension with the sole intention of causing trouble—those that used humans for whatever nefarious purposes they had in mind. Humans were a delicacy not only to vampires. This was where our supernatural army came into play; the ogres, werewolves, Hawks, witches and dragons that we had allied with.

One of the earliest problems that we successfully solved was the infestation of merpeople that plagued the coasts, making the beaches too dangerous to frequent. It was our dragons who helped with this, as they had once helped The Shade get rid of an infestation. We had a huge horde of dragons spend months in a row swimming along the coasts and devouring as many merpeople as they could. After four months of the dragons' nonstop assault, and God knew how many eaten merfolk, the merfolk became more cautious about roaming shallow waters and soon, they became a rare sighting. There were still reports of them causing trouble to boats and ships in deep water, but those complaints too were becoming less common.

The merfolk had apparently decided that the prospect of human flesh was not worth the risk of becoming a dragon's next meal. The dragons, of course, had been quite happy to do this job. Merfolk flesh was not their favorite food, but it was certainly not something they would turn down.

Another problem we'd managed to solve was intruding ogres. They mainly encroached in mountain regions, particularly in Canada. We'd had our army of allied ogres storm the worst-affected areas. They, too, were more than happy to do this job, for they had permission from their king Anselm to eat whatever ogres they found (I hadn't known ogres could descend into cannibalism). Food often seemed to be a good motivator for supernaturals.

Word soon spread among the rebel ogres, and they, like the mermaids, decided that it was no longer worth causing trouble on Earth. They soon chose to stick to the supernatural realm for food.

We also had a surprisingly large number of meddlesome werewolves who had taken up residence in huge swathes of forest. Ironically, the Mortclaws would have been good people for this job, had they been allied to us and still in their monstrous forms. They'd had a keen appetite for their own kind. But they had been cured of that tendency by Mona, and in fact, we no longer even knew where they were. Neither did Bastien. Apparently, they had been driven out of The Woodlands and forced to take shelter in some other distant place in the supernatural realm. So our army of werewolves worked together to drive out their meddlesome compatriots, along with the assistance of a team of witches.

We'd tried to work as strategically as possible to root out each and every major disturbance, and now the world was a far different place than it had been two years ago.

It was truly amazing how much Earth had changed in such a short amount of time. I had been expecting it to take far longer, but I supposed our success was simply a testament to what could happen under good leadership and when everybody worked together in harmony and cooperation.

Nowadays supernatural crime still existed, of course, but it was just like any other crime—whether it be among humans or supernaturals, evil existed everywhere. There was no escaping it. And that was what we at GASP were occupied with these days. We weren't away from The Shade nearly as much as we used to be. We had centers and agents all over the world who were trained in handling supernatural situations, and we still had clusters of our supernatural army to help out in various places—as well as witches on call when we needed them. After having been in the trenches getting our hands dirty for the past two years, now the majority of our work was strategy and high-level management, both of which we could do from home. Derek stalking about the living room in his blue checkered pajamas while in the midst of intense conversations with our agents was a daily sight in our home. It helped that as vampires we didn't need to sleep much. We could accommodate most time zones.

There were still occasions, however, when we were called out: for the most difficult cases. The cases that nobody else could solve.

We had received one such call yesterday, from Europe. The Greek island of Crete, to be precise. Strange happenings had been going on surrounding the archaeological site of Knossos. People—tourists and locals—going missing. Unexplained noises during the night. Vehicles mangled in odd ways.

Some superstitious locals were afraid that the Minotaur had returned from the hidden ruins of its labyrinth. I supposed I couldn't blame them for fearing this; when their eyes had been opened to so many other types of supernatural creatures over the past few decades, why rule out the Minotaur?

But yeah… I doubted we had a Minotaur on our hands. More likely it was some other kind of meddlesome supernatural.

Our troop was due to leave in a few hours' time.

I rolled over in our bed where I'd been trying to catch a bit of sleep before our departure. Derek was already up. And on the phone. I could hear his voice drifting from the kitchen.

I sat up, rubbing my eyes and stretching.

If there was one thing that I could say about this crazy life I was thrust into at the age of seventeen, it was that it never got boring.

Chapter 1: Grace

Lawrence had no idea how gorgeous he looked after a long day of skiing in the Alps. His locks of sandy blond hair were all mussed and touching the corners of his eyes as he pulled off his hat and goggles at the entrance to our log cabin. His lips and cheeks were still flushed, eyes alight and invigorated from the cold and the exercise.

As we piled into the hallway, we closed the door behind us to preserve our bungalow's warmth. Removing our boots, we slipped off our jackets and ski overalls and hung them over a radiator to dry.

This was our first day in the ski resort and I was

already feeling like we couldn't have chosen a better spot for our honeymoon. Moving into our living room, we stood together near the heater by the window, letting its warmth soothe our stretched muscles. Lawrence slipped an arm around my waist as we gazed out at the breathtaking view. We were perched fairly high up in the foothills, which afforded us enjoyment of the majestic peaks, as well as the rolling slopes of snowy white beneath us. This place held the magic of a winter wonderland even in the summer.

Darkness was falling upon the enchanting landscape and it had started to snow. Snowfall seemed like the perfect way to begin our night.

Lawrence leaned down to kiss my cheek. "Want something warm to drink?"

"Mmm," I murmured, closing my eyes and smiling against his kiss.

I followed him into the kitchen, where he fixed us some creamy hot chocolate. Then we returned to the living room where I knelt on the thick rug in front of the fireplace. I struck a match and used my fae powers to ignite the hearth until it crackled and emitted a divine halo of warmth. Then I resumed my seat on the cozy couch next to Lawrence and, after taking two sips from my hot chocolate, nestled against him. He gently ran a hand down my shoulder and along my right arm, leaving behind a trail of goosebumps.

Our cabin had a TV that could stream on-demand movies, but neither of us reached for the remote. The fire dancing in front of us and just being in each other's presence were all that we needed.

We had stopped for a meal in a cafeteria on the way back to our cabin from the slopes, so after finishing my mug of hot chocolate, I felt perfectly content.

I stretched out over Lawrence, resting my head against his knees. He glanced down at me with a warm smile.

"Ready to sleep?" he asked, a twinkle of mischief in his eyes.

"Um..." I caught a strand of his hair and twirled it round one finger. "Not quite yet."

After he'd swallowed the last of his hot chocolate, I draped one arm over his neck and eased him down so that I could taste his lips, still moist and sweet from his drink.

Then I rolled myself off of him and onto the chunky rug in front of the hearth, while catching his hand and pulling him down with me. As he crawled over me I felt the muscles beneath his shirt tensing. He engulfed my mouth before his lips spread their tender caress to the rest of my face, my nose, forehead, cheeks and then down the arch of my neck to the base of my throat.

My heartbeat quickening for him, I fumbled for his shirt buttons and undid them one at a time. Once I'd bared his torso, I gazed up at him, admiring the man I was now privileged to call my husband. Lawrence Conway, my hero and best friend.

I sat up, feeling the urge to take the lead in showering affection. We knelt on the rug while I landed kisses across his broad shoulders and collarbone. Then, leveling with his face, I let him wrap his arms around my waist, pull me closer and claim my lips.

With each stroke of his palms roaming my back beneath my shirt, and with each knead of his lips against mine, my heart felt warmer and warmer, fuller and fuller. It felt like it was ballooning within my chest, and there was no way I could adequately show how much love I felt for this man.

"I wish I could show you what I'm feeling," I whispered into his ear while his hands began to ease off my shirt.

"Show me, Grace," he breathed back, pulling my shirt off and discarding it on the floor by his own. He kissed me again intensely before raising his head. His tawny brown eyes were burning with desire as they roamed my face.

"It's impossible," I said, while arching my back to make room for his hands sliding beneath me and unclasping my bra. Then we removed each other's lower garments and stood together in the center of the rug, the fire glowing at our feet.

His hands cupped my cheeks and lifted my face so I could gaze into eyes. "Then let me try, Mrs. Conway," he whispered.

It felt like I was melting into his touch as we sank to our knees on the rug, and he laid me on my back. Running his hands down the back of my thighs and stopping beneath my knees, he parted my legs. Heat surged through me as he began to lower himself—gently and slowly at first—but his intense, glazed eyes locking with mine betrayed his passion. I caught his hands, twining my fingers through his, until he had descended near enough for me to reach his face. His body closing down on me—enveloping and folding me—I managed to breathe out his name before his lips captured mine.

Lawrence showed me his love deep into the night, while the snow outside fell thick and steady, and the hearth crackled with contentment. He showed me his love until I felt too full, too complete, to keep taking it from him, and I needed to take control so I could attempt to show him mine back.

As we woke the next morning on the ruffled rug, the embers beside us faded, our limbs coiled and entwined, it felt like last night had been our first time all over again. I supposed we had made a good start to showing what I believed could never truly be shown. But there was no rush. Lawrence and I still had the rest of our honeymoon to explore and discover… and then the rest of our lives.

Chapter 2: Hazel

"Murkbeech," I said through a mouthful of cereal. "The name hardly inspires."

I was paging through the brochure of the little Scottish island that my brother, Ruby, Julian, and I were supposed to be spending the next two weeks of our summer vacation on.

"It'll be much better than it sounds," my mother said from across the table as she topped up my glass of orange juice.

"Really?" my brother Benedict asked, his thick,

overgrown eyebrows rising. He sat to my left at the table, peering over my shoulder at the adventure island's promotional material. "Then how come you and Uncle Ben never wanted to go there? You preferred to escape to Hawaii."

My mother smirked as she rolled her eyes. "Your uncle Ben and I had already been to that island several years in a row. The first time we went, we enjoyed it. Just like you will. You'll make new friends. Go canoeing. Rock climbing. Learn how to survive in the wilderness. Plus, the center has been closed since last Christmas for renovation. They've upgraded the residences and introduced a whole bunch of new, exciting activities that weren't available when we attended the camp. You guys will be among the first group of teens to arrive on the island since they re-opened, so all the facilities will be squeaky clean and new."

"You should be their brand ambassador," Benedict muttered, biting into his toast.

Tired of my brother's dragon breath so close to

me—he had an annoying habit of waiting until after breakfast to brush his teeth—I pushed the brochure in front of him so that he no longer had to loom over me to see it.

"Do you know what time we're leaving?" I asked my mom.

She called over her shoulder, "Caleb, have you got news about the time yet?"

"Eight-fifteen," my dad called back from his and Mom's bedroom.

My mother glanced at the clock before her gaze returned to us. "That means you guys need to hurry up."

My mom was already dressed and ready. Her brown hair was tied back in a tight ponytail, and she wore her navy-blue GASP uniform. She looked kick-ass.

She and the rest of the members of GASP were heading off to Crete to solve a mystery, while my brother, Julian, Ruby and I—all humans—would be dropped off at Murkbeech Island along the way. If any of us were vampires already we would probably have been allowed to accompany them, except for Benedict, who was too young at fourteen, and Julian, who was fifteen. I was seventeen while Ruby was twenty. But as things stood, we were useless to GASP and would only pose a risk to their operations. We were expected to have a normal summer, just like any other human teenager.

I'd checked the weather in Scotland on the internet yesterday. It seemed pretty bad—cloudy and chilly and… murky. But apparently weather on that side of the world was never great, even in the summer. It was supposed to get a bit sunnier, though, over the next week.

Whatever the case, I preferred this kind of vacation to one lounging around on a beach in Hawaii. We already had a beach in The Shade, which I rarely frequented. Sun Beach had been more fun when I was a kid. These days, unless I was building an epic sandcastle with my friends or burying my brother in a sand grave, I found the beach boring. Yes, swimming was fun—to an extent. But it wasn't something I could do for hours, let alone days. And I wasn't a fan of sunbathing—neither was my skin. It was sensitive and broke out in a heat rash if I got too much sun. *A vampire in the making,* as my mother said.

Benedict and I quickly finished the last of our breakfast before we washed up and headed to our respective bedrooms. I had already packed my stuff the night before—well, at least most of it. And I had laid my clothes out on my bed: a pair of jeans, a comfy t-shirt and a baggy hoodie. I hurried to the bathroom and took a shower before returning to my room and getting dressed. I fixed up my hair in a messy bun, applied some lip balm, and then went about finalizing my luggage.

I rummaged through my bag—a tall, heavy-duty hiking backpack—checking that I hadn't forgotten anything. It contained primarily clothes, and wasn't completely full. We were supposed to travel with minimal stuff, because we would be given a bunch of survival gear when we arrived on the island that we'd need to carry around with us. Apparently we would be hiking all over the island, learning how to live in caves, find water, etc. And then toward the end we would be given a test to see if we could survive on our own for three days in a row, with no trainer or instructor present. We would be sorted into groups; I guessed that they would keep friends together, so Julian, Ruby, my brother and I would be together. But that was a call that the trainers would make, based on our various strengths and aptitudes for survival we showed throughout the course.

Once I had finished my final packing—including a few spare sets of socks, underwear, and an extra hoodie—I hurried to the music room and grabbed my flute from one of the shelves. I figured some music would be fun around the campfire.

Then came a knock at my door.

"Yeah?" I called.

My brother stepped inside, carrying his backpack. "Mom and Dad are waiting by the door. You ready?"

I zipped up my backpack and pulled it onto my back before giving him a firm nod. "Let's do this."

Chapter 3: Hazel

As we approached the clearing outside the Black Heights where GASP's giant helicopter was waiting, the first person I laid eyes on was Julian. He was standing next to his mother Ashley and father Landis, and was dressed in casual, comfy clothes, like Benedict and me. He looked sleepy—his brown eyes hazy behind his spectacles—and his tall, slim physique was hunched as he held his backpack.

"Hey, Jules!" Benedict called to him, as he and I approached with my parents.

"Hey," Julian croaked.

My parents greeted his parents—who were also dressed in GASP uniforms—while Benedict and I stood with Julian.

"Did you bring *Hell Raker IV?*" my brother asked, his eyes positively bulging with enthusiasm.

I grimaced. *Hell Raker IV* was a video game. Julian owned a portable video game console, which Benedict was obsessed with. Our parents had actually bought one for Benedict for his thirteenth birthday, but because of his inability to pry himself away from the device, they'd confiscated it less than two weeks later on the grounds that it was interfering with his school work.

Benedict's alternative was to leech off of Julian whenever he saw him.

"Yeah!" Julian responded. With only one year between them, they shared the same kiddish excitement whenever the subject of video games was broached.

Rolling my eyes, I returned my focus to the clearing, where dozens of GASP members were already climbing into the helicopter.

Then I spotted Ruby. Her blonde hair trailing down one shoulder in a braid, she was striding toward us with a smile on her face, her parents Claudia and Yuri by her side.

I strolled over to meet her.

"How're you doing?" I asked, grinning back at her.

"Excited," she said breathlessly. "Aren't you?"

"Yeah, I am." I glanced back over my shoulder at Julian and Benedict, who were now stooped over the console. "I'm sure glad you decided to come, though," I told her, "or I would've been stuck on the island with those two."

Ruby chuckled, shifting her backpack on her shoulders.

"Are you *sure* that's not too heavy for you?" Claudia asked, gazing up at her daughter in concern.

The height difference between Claudia and Ruby was quite comical. Ruby definitely took after her father in the height department.

"Yeah," Ruby said, sighing, "It's fine."

"She's a strong wee lass," Yuri said in a high, Scottish accent.

I snickered, as Claudia and Ruby rolled their eyes.

"My dad turned into a Scotsman the day he found out about our trip," Ruby muttered.

As we approached Julian's and my family, I couldn't help but notice Julian looking up from the game. His eyes passed over Ruby before he averted them. It seemed that girls were the one thing that could distract boys from video games, and Ruby was a girl Julian had obviously had a crush on for a while.

"All right, Julian?" Ruby asked with a friendly smile.

Julian nodded, coughing his throat clear. "Yeah."

Ruby didn't bother talking to my brother. He was lost in the world of Hell Raker. Whatever the heck that even was.

We headed together to the chopper and boarded it. Julian, Benedict, Ruby and I took seats near the back of the aircraft, opposite each other (myself next to Ruby, Benedict next to Julian) while the adults moved toward the front.

Once they were strapped in, the boys continued to busy themselves with the video game. I looked past Ruby—who was closest to the window—and gazed outside.

Folks were piling in quickly. I guessed we would be taking off in about ten minutes.

More often than not, when we needed to travel somewhere from The Shade, we went by the witches' magic. But I enjoyed traveling by aircraft. It was a nice change, and felt like more of an adventure. GASP usually took the chopper when they thought they might have to stay on-site for several days without returning to The Shade. The interior of the helicopter was designed to be converted into a sleeping area, and came with a fully stocked kitchen.

Ruby and I chatted until—fifteen minutes later—we took off. She went quiet after that. She suffered from airsickness, so she kept her eyes fixed firmly outside the window. We chatted for a bit once the aircraft had steadied, and then she decided to take a nap. She curled up beneath a blanket and fell into a light slumber, leaving me to either stare out of the window, watch the boggle-eyed boys in front of me, or… go on an adventure with my e-reader.

I stood up and opened the overhead compartment where we'd stuffed our bags. I slipped out the device I'd placed in one of the mesh side pockets for easy access. Resuming my seat, I switched it on and began scrolling through my library. I had a bunch of books I'd downloaded in anticipation for the trip… all of them romance novels. That was the good thing about e-readers—nobody knew what you were reading. Romance stories were my guilty pleasure. I'd always loved to read, but I had gotten hooked on romance in particular when my parents had gifted me an e-reader for my sixteenth birthday. Contemporary, human-only romance was my favorite genre—without any paranormal or fantasy elements. I had enough fantasy in my life already.

I found it endlessly interesting to live life through the eyes of a normal person, someone who hadn't grown up in The Shade. Though, thanks to all the supernaturals that had descended on Earth over the decades, you had to read the book descriptions carefully. Annoyingly, the contemporary and paranormal romance categories had all but merged.

After deciding on which book to read—a college sports romance—I reached into the pocket of my hoodie for my MP3 player and plugged myself in to some classical music. Music and reading… bliss. Both were a big part of my life outside of school.

Benedict was also into music. His main instrument was the trumpet. Yeah. That sure fit his character—at least when he was younger. He was becoming a bit more reserved in his old age.

Ruby woke up after a couple of hours and plugged into her own music player, while I remained immersed in my novel. It was about a football-playing hunk happening to fall for the plainest girl in the college. Maybe in all of America. Yeah, I had read tons of books with that cliché before but somehow, I hadn't gotten bored of it yet.

By the time we arrived, I'd managed to finish the book, along with two other novellas, as well as taking a nap.

As Kyle called out that we had reached our destination, I yawned and stretched out before standing up and pulling my bag from the overhead compartment. I replaced my e-reader in a mesh pocket, then pulled the bag onto my shoulders. I handed Ruby her bag, then did the same for Benedict and Julian. The four of us stood in the aisle as our parents and Corrine approached. There was no need for the whole aircraft to descend. They would stay in the air while the witch escorted us to the port, where we were due to meet with the adventure island's reps.

"You guys all ready?" my mother asked, looking each of us over.

"Yes," we replied.

I moved to the front of the aircraft with Benedict to say goodbye to my great-uncle Xavier and great-aunt Vivienne, along with my grandparents Sofia and Derek and great-grandpa Aiden.

Then we returned to gather around the witch, and the aircraft disappeared.

A chilly wind hit me as my feet landed on solid ground. The sky was dim and the atmosphere felt moist. We were standing in a narrow alleyway surrounded by high brick walls. I smelt the sea air—Corrine must've landed here to avoid us being spotted suddenly manifesting. Neither I, my brother, Ruby, or Julian were recognized by the public. And our parents wanted it to stay that way. So did we. We had signed up for the course with fake surnames to avoid being outed. We wanted this to feel like a normal vacation.

We moved to the end of the alley and peered around the corner, where a small port came into view. There was a large group of boys and girls our age already gathered there, each carrying big backpacks like us.

Our parents turned to us. My mom clutched my hands before pulling me in for a tight hug and kissing my cheek. Then my dad wrapped his arms around me and lifted me off my feet in a bearhug before kissing my forehead. After Benedict had his share of hugs and kisses, my mother said, "You both have your phones with you, right?"

My brother and I nodded.

"If there is anything at all that you need or want, call us. Your dad and I will keep our phones switched on at all times, and those phones are charmed so you can reach us when we return to The Shade. Otherwise we'll see you again in two weeks when we pick you up." She paused to grin. "Don't try to steal away to Hawaii or anything…"

"Yeah," I said. "Somehow I doubt we'll be doing that."

"Bye," Benedict said.

Our parents hugged us again, before allowing us to step away and out into view of the port. Julian and Ruby, who had finished saying goodbye to their parents, followed us. Each of us waved one final goodbye to all of our parents before crossing the road and approaching the crowd.

I knew that our parents wouldn't hang around for long to watch us leave, because they had a mission waiting for them.

The four of us walked instinctively close to each other as we arrived among the strangers. Many looked at us, examining us curiously before continuing with their various conversations.

Based on the accents I'd caught so far, most of these folks were from England, though there were some Scottish and a few Irish. I was sure that we would be the only people with American accents.

We moved toward the barrier that separated the dock from the water and formed a circle as we waited for our tour guides to arrive. Our eyes continued to wander over our fellow adventurers, whom we were going to be holed up with for the next two weeks.

Some appeared to have come on their own, and the fact that they stood solitary, not talking to anyone, suggested they had no friends, or at least none who had arrived yet.

But most had come in groups. Close to us was a

group of four girls with immaculate manicures, perfectly styled hair and full faces of makeup. I wasn't sure how they would fare marching through mud pits. Then there were duos and trios, some clearly siblings, others merely friends. The largest group consisted of ten boys—probably all from the same school. They looked around seventeen or eighteen, and judging by their accents they were definitely all from England. One guy in particular caught my eye. He spoke with a posh accent and appeared to be the center of attention, cracking all the jokes that the rest of the boys laughed at—a blond-haired, blue-eyed boy who could have very well popped out of a sports romance novel. In fact, he looked weirdly similar to the hunk I had just been reading about...

He seemed to sense me looking at him—or perhaps I'd just been gawking for too long—because his eyes rose to look at me directly. I quickly looked away, pretending that I hadn't been focused on him.

"Look," Benedict said, pointing toward the sea.

We turned to spot a ferry speeding toward us. At the front were a man and two women wearing matching uniforms: bright yellow jackets and pants. As they moved nearer, I could make out the words "Murkbeech Adventures" stamped on the jackets.

The crowd's attention turned to them as they stopped at the jetty. The reps leapt out of the boat and strolled toward us. The man and one of the women had fresh bright smiles on their faces, while the second woman looked unenthusiastic to say the least. Her expression was as gray as the clouds.

"Welcome, welcome, to Murkbeech, fellow adventurers!" the man boomed in a Scottish accent, clasping his hands together and addressing everyone with his unwaveringly broad smile. "Apologies, we're a wee bit late. But the good news is that every one of you should have arrived by now, so you shouldn't have to wait much longer."

I glanced down at my watch. They were only five minutes late. I had barely noticed.

"We're going to call out your names one by one,"

the cheerful woman said, producing a tall black register and a pen from her shoulder bag. "Please shout 'Aye!' when you hear your name."

She began to call us out in alphabetical order by first name.

Benedict was the first among the four of us to shout, "Aye!" Then, among a mix of other names, came me, Julian and Ruby. (Benedict's and my fake surname was "Donovan", Julian's was "Hersch", while Ruby's was "Stiller"—names Corrine had thought of off the top of her head).

The blond guy was the last to shout out. Wes Matthews was his name.

Wes... Hmm.

Then the second, moody woman spoke up for the first time. "I hope that we have not missed anyone?" At least, that was what I thought she'd said. Her accent was the thickest I'd ever heard, so thick it was hard to make out.

"My dad's Scottish accent really sucks compared to that woman's," Ruby said beneath her breath.

I let out a snort, a little louder than I had intended it to be.

The next thing I knew, the moody-looking woman had turned on me, her dull brown eyes sharpening. "I'm sorry," she said tersely. "Is something funny?"

I felt mortified as everyone's attention suddenly turned to me. I looked down at the ground and shook my head. "No, ma'am," I said.

She must've kept her gaze on me for a while, because the excruciating silence lasted for the next few seconds. Then the man came to my rescue and changed the subject.

"Well," he called out, "let's board the ferry!"

Ruby held my hand and squeezed it as the guides began leading us to the jetty and onto the ferry.

"She sure is a sour puss," Benedict mumbled.

I didn't raise my eyes until we had seated ourselves at the back of the ferry. Most people had hurried to the front, to get a better view of our destination, but I was happy to hang back for a while.

As we began to speed away from the port over the

choppy waves, it began to drizzle.

"Raincoats out!" the man announced cheerfully.

The four of us sighed as we stood up to rummage through our bags. Somehow, this didn't feel like the best start.

Chapter 4: Hazel

What had started out as a drizzle quickly turned into a downpour. It was hard to stay dry even with our raincoats. Luckily our bags were waterproof, so none of our stuff got ruined, though I was forced to relocate all of the objects in the side mesh pockets into the inside compartments.

The ferry was open-air, with not even the thinnest covering to shelter us. Rather stupid if you asked me, for somewhere with weather as volatile as Scotland. But maybe they did it on purpose, to give us our first taste of "raw" life. Which meant that things were about to get a lot rawer.

Although the ground was slippery, and the boat incredibly bumpy from being rocked about by the strong waves, the four of us were tired of hanging around near the back of the vessel. Slowly but surely, we milled through the crowd toward the front, in an attempt to get a better view.

We slid as close to the front row as we could physically reach. I was just about to grip hold of the side of the boat for support and secure the position I had found for myself when a girl in front of me stepped backward unexpectedly, causing me to lose balance. Slipping backward on the wet floor, I braced myself for a butt-fall, but it didn't come to that. I fell back against someone. Into someone. Arms looped through mine, catching me and setting me back on my feet.

Strong arms.

As I turned around to glimpse my savior… it was Wes.

Oh, my God. This is like the biggest cliché of all time!

I felt the heat rise to my cheeks.

"I'm sorry," I managed.

His handsome face broke out in a smile, his blue eyes—boy, they really were gorgeous up close—warming. He even had dimples, dammit.

"No problem," he said, in his dreamy British accent. "Might want to get a hold of the side while you can now, though," he added.

He was close enough for me to smell his crisp cologne, and his breath—a nice minty scent.

"Yeah," I said vaguely, reaching out and gripping the side of the boat, as I swallowed.

I was expecting him to drift away back into the crowd from whence he had materialized… but no. He stood next to me. And his eyes remained on me.

"You're American," he remarked.

"Yeah," I said again, my insides turning to mush.

"Whereabouts in America?"

"Uh, California." That was rather an outdated answer. It was one that my mother and uncle used to use—only they could legitimately say that they had lived in America. They had spent the first five years of their life in California. I couldn't say I had, but it was the best response I could give without revealing my identity.

"Cool," he said. "Surprised you came all this way though…" His brows rose.

"Well, this place was recommended by friends of my parents," I replied, wincing internally as my lie deepened.

"Must've been a high recommendation," he muttered.

"Whereabouts are you from, exactly?" I asked, turning the focus on him.

"Oxford," he replied.

"Oh. Cool."

"You're here with friends?" he asked.

"With my brother and two friends, yes." I gestured toward them, as I avoided my brother's eye contact. I knew that he was going to do something stupid like wink or stick his tongue out at me, something I really did not need to see in this moment.

"I'm here with classmates," Wes offered. "Went to boarding school together. We're all eighteen and will be starting university after the summer—most of us going in different directions. This trip is a kind of final get-together for us… How old are you?"

"Seventeen," I replied.

"I see." His eyes turned away from me to look ahead. "Looks like we're arriving," he said.

Sure enough, the outline of a rocky island was manifesting in the distance through the sheets of rain.

"Hey, Wes! Get over here!" one of his friends called from the other side of the crowd.

Wes looked at me again, flashing me another pearly smile. "I'll catch you later, I guess."

"Yeah," I said.

I gazed after him as he left me and crossed the deck toward his group of friends.

My three companions, who'd kept their distance from me while Wes had been by my side, moved toward me. My brother's face was plastered with a grin that would have rivaled the Cheshire Cat's, while Julian and Ruby were also looking at me in amusement.

Ruby nudged me in the shoulder. "He ain't bad now, is he?"

I shook my head, my brain still recovering from his presence, my heartbeat gradually resuming its normal pace.

Man. I need to stop reading so many romance novels.

Chapter 5: Hazel

The ferry slowed to a stop as we reached a tiny port. Our guides bundled us off the boat and onto the jetty, where we ascended a long trail of stone steps up to a picturesque little town. We passed through a square that held a total of three shops—a general store, a grocery and a gift shop—and a cafe that overlooked the few boats moored by the jetty. As I gazed around, this clearly was more of a village than a town. And the people looked as moody as the weather—or that female guide who'd snapped at me. A few of them peered at us through shop windows darkly, like we were unwelcome intruders. I wondered whether they had been like this even in my mother's time. Maybe over the years they'd gotten tired of hordes of rowdy teenagers interrupting their peace.

We ventured down several cobblestone lanes lined on either side by quaint cottages, until we reached a pebbly parking lot. A large bus waited in one corner with the same logo as the guides' jackets stamped across it:

"MURKBEECH ADVENTURES."

At least we could board a vehicle here and weren't expected to traipse our way to the facility. We left our bags on the ground for the guides to stow into the large luggage compartment in the belly of the vehicle.

Benedict, Ruby, Julian and I managed to board the bus first. We headed straight for the backseats (Julian suggesting that Ruby sit by the window since she suffered from travel sickness in general). I peered out of the window as I spotted Wes climbing aboard. He sat near the front with his friends.

The engine rumbled to a start. The bus pulled out and swerved onto a narrow road that wound close to the coast. I looked through the back window and watched the small scatter of buildings that made up the village fade into the distance. Then I looked back out of Ruby's window at the mass of churning gray water. Another small island loomed, perhaps ten miles away. That was apparently owned by the adventure company, and nobody inhabited it but animals. It was meant for wilderness survival training, something we were supposed to be starting over the next few days.

Other than the road, which quickly turned into a dirt track, all signs of human civilization on this island were evaporating too. We wound deeper and deeper into nature, passing rolling green hills grazed by wild goats, until the route became gravel and a building came into view—a sprawling one-story building with a brown tile roof and walls of dark wooden panels.

"Welcome to Murkbeech," read the sign above the oaken front entrance.

It definitely looked like it had been newly

renovated. No stains on the building. "Squeaky clean," as my mom would say.

The doors to the bus ground open and we began piling out. Being at the very back, Ruby, Julian, my brother and I were the last to climb out. I pulled my hoodie closer to me against the cool breeze. After reclaiming our bags, we were herded into the building.

A rush of warm air engulfed us, which was a relief. At least this place wasn't too basic to have central heating. The building smelt like fresh paint and woodchips.

The guides—who had introduced themselves as Peter, Suzanne and Gillian (the grumpy one) by now—handed each of us a square card with a number before pointing the girls and boys in separate directions; the girls' residence was to the left of the building, the boys' to the right. I supposed that was sensible.

Gillian followed the girls down the hallway toward the female quarters, showing us to our rooms.

Oddly, her mood had done a hundred-and-eighty-degree turn. I could no longer call her grumpy. Her previously glum face was now all smiles as she cheerfully helped confused or lost girls find their doors. She even flashed *me* a smile as we walked past.

I frowned.

"Maybe she's got PMS or something," Ruby said once we got out of earshot.

"Hm." I shrugged, brushing thoughts of her away as we arrived in our dormitory. It contained three bunkbeds—six mattresses in total, four of which were already taken by the group of four girls with spotless manicures I'd noticed earlier. As Ruby and I entered the room, their eyes roamed us briefly before they turned their backs and resumed their conversation. Clearly they weren't interested in getting to know us, but that was fine by Ruby and me.

Ruby offered me first dibs on the bunks, and I chose the top one. We dumped our bags on the floor, and, after peeling off our raincoats, hung them on the hooks on the back of the door.

Then we headed out of the dorm in search of the communal bathrooms. We found them at the end of our corridor, jam-packed with girls taming their hair and blow-drying it after the downpour, or looking in the mirror to retouch their makeup. Makeup was the very last thing I'd thought to bring on this trip.

After Ruby and I used the toilets, we returned to our dorm. We spent the next fifteen minutes unpacking a few things; we really didn't want to unpack much. We were only here for two weeks, and besides, we would need most of the stuff in our bags when we ventured out for the survival course.

Ten minutes later, a shrill bell sounded in the corridor outside.

"Gather around, everybody! It's time for the welcome meeting in the living room." It was Gillian's voice, still cheerful.

We left the room, following after the four girls who had redone their hair and applied spritzes of overwhelming perfume.

We waited in the hallway as Gillian finished gathering all the girls and then we headed back the way we came, toward the entrance. But this time we strode through a set of double doors directly opposite the main door to the building. We emerged in a large but cozy communal sitting area. Long bouncy sofas were spread generously about the room, along with armchairs, oversized cushions, and thick fluffy rugs covering the wooden floors. In one corner was a massive fireplace, in front of which sat a rocking chair.

Many of the boys were already here. We spotted Julian and my brother, who had a sofa to themselves. They were playing with Julian's console while they waited. Ruby and I took seats next to them.

As I continued surveying the room, I tried to convince myself that I was not looking for Wes, but that would've been a lie. I spied him taking a seat a few sofas away, with his band of friends.

Once the room had almost reached the point of standing room only, it seemed that everybody had arrived, boys and girls. Five guides had entered the room and stood by the fireplace, where all of the couches faced.

Gillian, Suzanne and Peter were with two other men who were clearly twins. They wore the same cheerful yellow uniform as their colleagues and introduced themselves as Charlie and Jamie.

"I would like to welcome you all once again to Murkbeech." Peter spoke up, his eyes traversing the room. "It is an honor to receive you as guests here, and we're sure that you all will thoroughly enjoy your stay."

He went on to repeat much of what I had already read in the brochure, the history of the center's founding, how it had been running the last fifty years, and had equipped countless young adults with essential survival skills as well as memories that would last a lifetime.

"There has never been a more exciting time to visit Murkbeech. As many of you know, we recently renovated the hostel and our equipment, as well as planned many new adventure activities that you will have the opportunity to participate in during your trip." He rubbed his hands together. "So, if nobody has any questions, we will get right to the good stuff! You only have two weeks with us and we're going to ensure that you make the most of every single day. No slackers here, right?" Although he received some less-than-enthusiastic looks from the young adults surrounding him, he grinned as he looked around and continued, "Tomorrow, we will head to Durrow Island. I'm sure that many of you spotted it through the bus window on our way here. We will be leaving early. Breakfast is at 8 AM and everyone must be ready to walk out the door by 9:30 AM—and make sure you wear your swimsuits beneath your clothes. We'll be heading to the center's private port, on this side of the island, where we'll take a boat."

"When will we go horseback riding?" one of the younger girls called out.

"Toward the end of the trip," the man replied. "Relaxing stuff like horseback riding, canoeing, etc, will be saved for the end. You need to earn it first!"

"What exactly will we be doing tomorrow?" a boy a few seats in front of us asked.

"We'll be embarking on a trek across Durrow Island… That's all I'll say for now. It'll be a surprise!"

Two more male staff entered the room carrying a massive black bag. They planted it in front of Peter and unzipped it. It was filled with white cloth bags.

"Here we have some equipment that you'll need to bring with you. I want to ask you to form a line around the room so we can hand these out one by one."

Everyone was given their own white bag. We returned to our sofa to examine their contents. Each bag contained a Swiss army knife, a lighter, a flashlight, and a ball of sturdy string, as well as a bunch of other bits and pieces.

"Pack what we've given you in your hiking backpacks, along with enough clothing for five days," Peter said.

"What about food?" another boy asked.

"Don't worry about that, dear," Suzanne said. "We'll take care of it."

"Are there toilets on that island?" one of the four snooty girls asked.

At this, all of the guides chuckled. "No," Charlie said. "You'll be roughing it."

His statement was met with a mixed response, both laughter and disgust. I just made a mental note to bring toilet paper…

"You have the rest of the evening off to explore the hostel and the grounds. Just don't venture past the fences without permission. We'll meet again for dinner—the dining room is through that door." He pointed to a door at the back of the sitting room, from which an aromatic smell was already emanating. "And after you've eaten, there will be a little surprise."

Everyone stood up and began leaving the room. Most headed back to the dorms, while others made their way out of the main entrance. It had stopped raining, and the sky seemed to have cleared up.

The four of us returned to our rooms to grab some warm clothes before meeting again by the entrance. We ventured outside into the cool evening and gazed around. The horizon glowed orange from the descending sun. I breathed in the crisp sea air as I zipped up my jacket and wrapped a scarf around my neck.

We crossed the gravelly parking area and entered the hilly grassland that surrounded the hostel. We trudged to the nearest hill within the boundary of the wooden fence that ran in a wide circle around the building, and gazed out at the view of the choppy sea and Durrow Island beyond.

"Look, there are the horses," Julian pointed out. East of the island were a couple of large stables. Horses roamed a grazing area attached to it. A few people had gathered around to pet the animals and feed them grass.

We wandered around the grounds a little longer, away from everyone else, until the sun had disappeared. There were no lights at all in this area other than those emanating from the building. It was almost time for dinner anyway so we headed back. We made our way straight to the dining room, like most of the others who'd been outside. It was a long white-walled room with steel tables and fluorescent lighting. There was a canteen at one end where members of staff were already laying out food.

By the time everyone had assembled and we were given permission to start helping ourselves, my stomach was rumbling. After piling up my plate, I dug into the meal until I couldn't take another bite. Leaning back in my chair, I watched Ruby, Julian and Benedict finishing their meal. They must have been hungry too because they finished shortly after I did.

As people began standing to leave, Peter requested we wait for a while in the sitting room for a "surprise". We sat down on the same sofa we had occupied earlier and watched the fire crackling in the hearth.

After the dining room had emptied, a short plump woman with large round spectacles and a mop of wild curly hair entered the sitting room. She was wearing navy blue corduroy pants and a floral-patterned shirt. She walked to the rocking chair in front of the fire and slid into it.

"Good evening." She spoke up, looking around the room. Her Scottish accent was no less thick than Gillian's. "I am Mrs. McKenzie, owner of Murkbeech Adventures, and before you go to sleep tonight—as is the tradition for all new arrivals on our island—I would like to tell you a welcome story…"

Someone dimmed the lights, leaving only the crackling fire to illuminate the room. The firelight reflected in Mrs. McKenzie's spectacles as she began to recount a spooky story. She wouldn't tell us whether it was true or not, but it was a tale about a young woman who had committed suicide on Durrow Island almost a century ago. She had been living on the mainland before receiving news that her sailor husband had perished on an expedition. The very night she was informed about his death, she took a boat and sailed across the perilous waters to the deserted Durrow Island, where she tied a noose around her neck and hanged herself from the tallest tree. According to Mrs. McKenzie, to this day, you could sometimes hear the bough creaking, as if a heavy weight were pulling it down, and an anguished cry mingling with the howls of the wind…

Her story ended with the slamming of a door, causing several of the younger teens to scream. It was a sound effect courtesy of Peter, who stood silhouetted in the doorway, his arms crossed over his chest.

"Well, time for bed!" Mrs. McKenzie shrilled. "Durrow Island awaits you in the morning…"

Peter turned the lights back on as people began to leave the sitting room. Standing up, I yawned and stretched out. My hand brushed against someone accidentally. I quickly withdrew, before realizing that it was Wes whom I had brushed against.

"Sorry," I breathed, for what would be the second

time that day.

Wes flashed me a smile. "Sleep tight, Hazel," he said, before disappearing out of the room.

Chapter 6: Hazel

I hoped that Mrs. McKenzie's story wouldn't prevent my brother from sleeping that night. As grown-up as he liked to think he was, he was still a kid in my eyes. At home, he still slept with a nightlight. At least he was sharing a dorm with Julian, who could be like an older brother.

I wasn't afraid of ghosts, given all that I knew about them. Heck, my uncle (and great-uncle) had been a ghost once. There wasn't a lot that could scare me, considering that I lived on an island filled with creatures that went bump in the night…

I couldn't deny, though, that I found Mrs. McKenzie's story creepy. It didn't help that I was sleeping in a strange place. I never slept well the first time I arrived in a new location and this night was no exception. I tossed and turned in my bed for an hour trying to fall asleep and in the end, my hand ended up slipping into my bag and retrieving my e-reader. I relapsed into my guilty habit.

I must've read until I was unconscious with exhaustion, because when I woke up, it was to find my e-reader lying against my chest, the tall light by my bedside still switched on. The morning sun streamed through the curtains.

The four girls we shared the dorm with were still asleep, but it seemed that Ruby was awake. I felt her shifting on the bottom bunk.

"How did you sleep?" I whispered, rubbing my eyes.

"Not too well," Ruby replied, her voice deep and thick.

I checked my watch. Realizing that I had forgotten

to adjust the time zone, I looked at the clock above the door. It was already seven forty-five. Breakfast was served in fifteen minutes.

As Ruby and I gathered a fresh set of clothes and our swimwear, I suggested that we wake the girls. We approached them reluctantly and shook their bed frames.

"Hey," I said. "Time to wake up."

They slowly rose to consciousness, grumbling. Ruby and I headed to the bathrooms to take a shower and dress. They were packed, as was to be expected. By the time we returned, the girls were already clothed for the day. Apparently they'd decided to skip washing this morning.

Breakfast was a simple affair. There wasn't a lot to choose from, just porridge, cereals, and fresh fruit. I was still feeling stuffed from the night before, but I wasn't sure what kind of food we would be eating over the next few days when we roamed Durrow Island, so I stocked up as much as I could.

Benedict and Julian looked sleepy as they joined

Ruby and me at our table.

I didn't need to ask how their night had been. Not great, like us.

"Good morning," Suzanne said, striding to the canteen and addressing everybody. She was looking dull and unsmiling compared to yesterday. "I have a request for you all to please leave your phones in your dormitories. Bringing any sort of modern equipment with you will simply detract from your time here and work against what we're trying to get you to experience."

Her words were met with a negative response. For most people, having their phones pried from them was like having to part with a kidney. People had become so dependent on phones these days. I couldn't say I was. I didn't like being dependent on any particular object or device… except my little e-reader.

After breakfast, we returned to the dorms and packed up our bags. Removing my phone from my backpack, I recorded a special voicemail for my parents in case they called, explaining where we were and why I wasn't taking the phone with me. Ruby did the same for her parents.

Then we made our way to the sitting room and waited for everyone else to gather around.

As we sat, I couldn't help but notice our four roomates sidle over to Wes and his group—Wes was looking particularly handsome with mussed hair and a slightly dazed, sleepy look in his eyes.

The girls started engaging in what was clearly flirting with the guys, one of the girls talking to Wes directly. Apparently, at some point between yesterday and today, they had managed to establish a rapport.

Not that I cared. At all.

Swallowing, I shifted my focus to the door, waiting not so patiently for the guides to arrive and escort us to Murkbeech Adventures' private port.

They didn't keep us waiting long. Everyone was pretty punctual and soon we were leaving the hostel and hiking across the grassland toward the boundary fence.

The port wasn't far away, if it could even be called a port. It was just a small wooden jetty where a single boat was moored. Another open-air boat. *Sea Breeze* was its name.

The guides, who were carrying backpacks larger and heavier than the rest of us, piled in first and started the boat, while we boarded.

We took seats and watched as we moved away from the jetty and into the waters, which were choppier than I had expected them to be on such a fine day. There wasn't a cloud in the sky, so very different from the weather the day before. Hopefully, the good weather would hold up for as long as we were on the island. There would be plenty of other obstacles to contend with without worrying about rain.

The girls continued to suck up to Wes and his crew throughout the journey. Not that I was looking their way... Particularly.

I focused on Durrow Island, gradually looming

closer and closer.

It was hard to estimate how big it was—not terribly big, but big enough to get lost in.

True to the spirit of this adventure course, Julian confirmed that he had left behind his game console when I asked him. That was pretty good of him and Benedict both. They might've left their phones behind, but I'd been expecting them to still bring their toy for whatever downtime we had. I supposed it would run out of batteries pretty quickly anyway and there was no electricity on the island.

The four of us were the first to debark as the boat pulled into a tiny dock. We leapt to the ground and stared back at Murkbeech Island, now a vague outline in the distance.

Everybody looked pretty nervous as they gazed around at our new destination, or what we could see of it so far. White cliffs, sludgy grassland and pebbly beaches.

Once everybody was out of the boat, the guides led us away from the shore and onto the mainland.

We followed a narrow trail through the puddle-filled grass until the ground began to ascend and I realized that they were leading us up to one of the cliffs. It wasn't long before everybody was panting. The sun started to feel unpleasantly warm. I tore off my jacket and tied it around my waist while fanning myself with my hands.

That was when I realized I'd forgotten to pack sunblock. *Crap.* On asking Julian, Ruby and Benedict, they had forgotten too. I burnt easily in the sun, even in the morning. By the end of the day, if the sun kept up its intensity, my face would be as red as a tomato.

I continued to peel off my layers the higher we climbed; after my jacket I removed my sweater, and then my shirt, until I was just wearing a tank top. Even still, my back felt sweaty, so I rolled it up, letting the breeze touch my midriff.

My face got a bit warmer still as one of the girls sped up to walk beside Wes.

Then I spotted a tube of sunblock in his hands.

He was applying it to his face and the back of his neck.

"Hey, Wes," I called out, suddenly experiencing a surge of unexpected boldness. He turned as I reached him, his eyes falling briefly to my bare midriff before returning to my face.

I ignored the way the brunette girl was sizing me up as I pointed to the sunblock and asked Wes, "Could my friends and I borrow some of that?"

"Sure," he said, handing me the bottle.

I remained walking by his side as I squeezed out some of the lotion into my right hand and began applying it to my face, arms, midriff, and any other part of my skin that was exposed to the sun.

Then I handed it to Ruby.

"The sun bothers you?" Wes asked. He must have noticed how much discomfort I was in. Nobody else reacted quite as strongly as I did, not even my three Shade companions. "That must be a bummer in California."

I laughed dryly.

Julian, who was the last to use the sunblock, handed it back to Wes, thanking him.

The brunette slipped back and rejoined her friends with a slight scowl on her face after seeing all of Wes's focus switched to me. None of us had much breath to talk though for the next few hours as we continued scaling the mountain.

When we finally reached the top, I had a stitch in my side and my calf muscles ached. We took a break for water and a light snack of a granola bar as we admired the view from the cliff top. I had to say that it was worth the climb. Truly stunning. We were able to see the extent of Murkbeech from this height; I could just about make out some details, too—the hostel toward the west coast, and the tiny village and port on the east side.

Benedict slumped down on the grass, using his clunky backpack for support as he leaned backward.

"Ugh," he grumbled. "I wish I was a supernatural."

I eyed him sharply, while a girl to our left giggled,

a girl I'd barely noticed until now. She was a bright-faced girl with a short black bob complete with low-hanging bangs that almost covered her light blue eyes. She looked no older than fourteen.

Benedict's eyes shot toward her... and then he blushed.

Now it was my turn to grin. *Oh, this is precious.*

"What's your name?" I asked her.

"Carrie," she replied.

"Cool," I said. "I'm Hazel, and this is my brother Benedict. How old are you?"

"Fourteen in September."

Even cooler.

"That's awesome," I said. "Benedict was hoping to make a friend closer to his own age on this trip."

The blush in Benedict's cheeks intensified. He cast me a mortified look.

I turned my back on the two of them and faced Ruby... only to find her in conversation with one of Wes's friends.

"Okay, folks! Let's keep moving!" Suzanne called.

Benedict was already standing up and hurrying to Julian's side, apparently too shy to hold a conversation with Carrie, in spite of her friendliness.

We began descending the mountain in a different direction—south, and deeper into the center of the island. Descending was a lot more fun than ascending. In addition to having gravity as our aide, this side of the mountain was shady. Soon I was rolling down my tank top and putting on my shirt again.

We spent the next few hours roaming through mostly flatland, though it was punctuated with water holes, which didn't make for easy walking.

Once 2 p.m. arrived, I was more than ready for lunch. I was still worried about exactly what we were going to be doing for food, but Gillian, still in a cheery mood, explained. (Peter was still in a quiet mood, which was odd given that he had been the most enthusiastic among the guides when we first arrived.) Gillian said that she and her fellow guides were carrying enough long-life food for all of us for the next three days, but after that we were going to have to rely on scavenging our own food for meals. They would train us how to find everything that was edible on this island, along with how to prepare and cook it. Water, however, we would have to start locating by tomorrow morning, because it was impractical to carry such a large amount for all of us, especially due to the rate at which we were drinking with all this sun and exercise.

We stopped at some rocks at the base of a hill, where the guides handed us sandwiches. We wolfed them down, and then it was time to keep moving.

"The caves where we will sleep tonight are located on the other end of the island," Suzanne explained. "And, given that there's no electricity here, we have to reach there before dark. So we can't afford to dally."

"You *definitely* don't want to be caught out here after dark," Jamie added in a spooky voice.

I shuddered recalling Mrs. McKenzie's story and found myself wondering where that tree was where the widow was supposed to have hanged herself—assuming any of the story was true at all.

After another hour of trekking, we arrived at the border of a wide lake. It stretched out on either side of us for miles.

I was expecting us to begin walking around it, but our guides had other plans.

"The fastest way to the caves is straight ahead," Charlie said. He pointed directly across the lake.

"You're saying that we have to swim?" one of the boys asked.

"I am indeed," Charlie replied with a grin.

"What?" I couldn't help but splutter. "But what will we do with our bags? We won't be able to take them with us. They'd get ruined!"

"That's why we must build a raft," Jamie said.

Oh, man.

Jamie took us to a nearby stretch of trees, where there was, conveniently, a lot of fallen logs. Thick ones too. Perhaps they'd been placed here in advance so that we wouldn't have to actually start felling the trees. If we did have to do that, God knew how much time it would take. I doubted we would make it to the caves by nightfall.

The guide instructed us to drag the wood to the edge of the lake, and then we used the string we carried to tie them all together until we'd formed a wide raft, large enough to hold all of our stuff. My back was aching by the time we finished. I stood up straight, stretching, my forehead moist with a sheen of sweat from the sun that still beat down upon us.

Suzanne pulled out a thicker rope from her bag and tied it to the middle of the front of the raft. Then we all worked together to push the raft into the lake, which was freezing cold.

Luckily, the lake wasn't as long as it was wide. I guessed that it would take us maybe ten or fifteen minutes of swimming to get to the other side of it.

We carefully cooperated to load all of our bags on top of the raft before it was time for us to get into the water.

"I suggest you strip to your swimwear," Suzanne

said, as she and the guides began tearing off their clothes and laying them upon the rafts to keep them dry.

Amidst grumbling, most of us removed our clothes and placed them on the raft, except for a few more self-conscious people who decided to swim with their clothes on. After we had all removed our shoes and stowed them near our bags, we ventured into the lake.

My body broke out in shivers as I immersed myself to my knees. Then I leapt in fully.

I caught sight of Wes entering a few feet away from me. My eyes roamed his toned chest before I focused straight ahead on the other side of the lake.

We took it in turns to pull the raft by the rope Suzanne had attached to it, though, as I had guessed, it wasn't a long swim. I didn't end up getting a chance to pull it even if I'd wanted to.

We arrived on the other side and hurried out of the water, our bare feet sinking into the porous ground.

We pulled the raft onto land and collected our respective clothing and shoes. I dove into my bag for a towel and dried myself off, but there was only so far I could dry my swimwear, so, after putting on my shoes, I was forced to wait a while.

Some others put on their clothes anyway, but most had the same idea as me, including Wes, who was making his way toward me now. The muscles in his chest flexed as he walked.

I found myself short of breath as his eyes traveled the length of me. I felt like I might as well not be wearing anything at all.

"Let's keep moving!" Suzanne shrilled, to my relief.

Yes, let's.

***

I was loath to say that the view from the caves was worth all the hassle we'd gone through to get here… but it would have been a lie to say that it wasn't. We reached the caves just as the sun was dipping in the sky. They were located—to my surprise—right on the beachfront, affording us an unrivaled view of the sea. The waves glimmered in the fading evening light, creating a deep sense of calm, peace after a hectic day.

We still had work to do though. Quite a bit of work before darkness engulfed us.

We set up our stuff in a deep cave, which was thankfully dry, and spread out our sleeping bags in rows. Benedict, Julian, Ruby and I set up near the entrance so that we wouldn't have to trip over a load of people if we needed to relieve ourselves during the night. I had been holding myself in all day, dreading the moment when I would have no choice but to venture out and find somewhere to squat.

Next, we were tasked with collecting kindling to start a fire. The guides had brought a large pot with them, as well as sachets of instant soup.

Within the white bags they had handed us before we left were light aluminum cups and spoons, which I supposed we would be eating with.

After we collected the wood and piled it near the entrance of the cave on the sand, the guides demonstrated how to light a fire with two sticks. Ten minutes later, we found ourselves all sitting around it in a circle, our eyes going hazy from the smoke as it rose higher and higher, until we had before us a full-fledged bonfire.

The guides placed a large pot containing water and the sachets over the fire.

"When we go looking for water tomorrow," Jamie explained, "we'll head up this mountain." He pointed directly above us at the looming cliffside. "There are a bunch of pure streams that run near the top, with the most delicious water you've ever tasted. I guarantee it."

By the time we'd finished our soup, it was dark. The firelight was the only source of light other than the moon and stars. It was a beautifully clear night.

I noticed Peter retreating into the cave as soon as he finished his meal, his head hung low.

I eyed Suzanne, who was sitting closest to me.

"Is Peter okay?" I dared to ask.

Suzanne shrugged. "Why wouldn't he be?"

"Well, he just seems a lot more quiet than before."

She frowned, and looked back toward the cave he had disappeared into, but made no further comment.

I was soon distracted from the subject by Wes, who, along with his friend whom I'd spotted talking to Ruby earlier, came to sit by Ruby and me.

I fell into a conversation with Wes and he started asking me about my hobbies. I was tempted to fetch my flute, but I felt a bit too shy to start playing amidst such new acquaintances. Maybe tomorrow night or the next. We still had plenty of days to go on this trip. I would find ample opportunity.

I kept glancing at Carrie, who sat opposite us. She threw a look at Benedict every once in a while, but it seemed that he was deliberately ignoring her.

He let out a loud sigh and, shoving his cup and spoon away, leaned backward. As he stretched out his legs, Suzanne snapped, "What are you doing, stupid boy?"

Benedict jolted at the admonition and quickly withdrew his legs. Alarmed, I broke off my conversation with Wes and stared at her. Suzanne, like Peter initially, had been nothing but smiles since we'd arrived... I was quite shocked by the way her expression had contorted with not just irritation, but anger.

"Sorry," Benedict mumbled. Shaken, he backed himself further away from the fire.

His legs hadn't even been that close. Not nearly close enough to be dangerous. I would've warned him if they had.

As I exchanged a disconcerted glance with Ruby, I couldn't help but wonder if these tour guides were on something...

Chapter 7: Hazel

We retreated to our sleeping bags soon after Suzanne had snapped. I fell asleep much sooner than I had expected to. I supposed that the exhaustion of the day, and being surrounded by fresh air even while I lay in the cave, had worn me out.

But I woke up with a start at three a.m. As my eyes pried open, and I found myself staring at the roof of the cave, I was immediately confused as to where I was. Then I remembered. Yeah, we had really gone through with this Scottish adventure thing.

I realized that it was the sound of sobbing that had woken me up.

I sat up slowly, my eyes adjusting to the gloom of the cave, as I tried to make out where the noise was coming from.

I fumbled for my flashlight and switched it on. It didn't sound like a female, but a male. I stood up. Everyone else seemed to be asleep. Or at least most people. Ruby, Benedict and Julian were snoring, but I spotted a few others toward the back of the cave lying awake and staring up at the ceiling, a couple of them whispering. But nobody seemed to be reacting to the sobs.

Having a younger brother of my own, I couldn't just ignore them. I moved to the entrance of the cave, which was where the noises were originating from. It was then that I realized that the sobbing wasn't coming from a boy at all. It was coming from a full-grown man. Peter. He too had found a spot near the entrance to sleep, and now he was lying on his side, facing the sea.

His eyes were clamped shut, his lips trembling as he continued to make whimpering noises.

I felt extremely awkward and uncomfortable witnessing a grown man act like a young boy. He didn't seem to be awake. He appeared to be having some kind of traumatic nightmare.

I was about to make my way back to my sleeping bag and try to forget what I'd seen when he started speaking in low whispers. So low that I had to bend down to his level to make out what he was saying.

"No, please don't come again. Don't come again. You're not welcome back here!"

My breath hitched at the sheer terror in his tone.

What is he seeing in his mind's eye?

I was tempted to shake him awake and ask him, but that would've been pretty rude, considering that I barely even knew him. I listened to him for the next few minutes, repeating the same chilling words, until he quieted down. And then his sobbing stopped. He fell back into a slumber, his chest heaving up and down.

***

I'd lost all chances of falling back to sleep that night—at least, deep sleep. I was forced to go relieve myself at four a.m., and then managed to drift off into a semi-slumber as the morning progressed. I also developed a dull headache, either due to lack of sleep, or the cool air.

Ruby was the first of my companions to wake up. She sat up abruptly, wide-eyed. I could see that she experienced the same bout of confusion I had earlier.

"Ugh," she said huskily, rubbing her forehead, then her throat. "I think I caught a chill in the night." She swallowed gingerly.

"I've got a headache," I said.

"Yeah, me too."

I glanced toward Peter's direction. He was still asleep, like most of the others in the cave. Then I told Ruby about his sobs and whispering.

"Guess he must have had a really bad dream," she murmured.

"Yes," I said. "That's what I told myself."

When Julian and Benedict woke up, they'd also

developed some kind of mild head cold. It was probably a mistake that all four of us had slept so close to the entrance of the cave. We would have been more sheltered from the wind toward the back.

I told Julian and my brother about what I'd witnessed with Peter. Benedict looked spooked, while Julian shrugged and basically repeated what Ruby had said.

Being among the first awake, we moved out of the cave toward the waves, where we brushed our teeth and freshened up. On our return, most of the cave was awake. As we returned to our sleeping bags, my eyes were on Peter. He was sitting upright, gazing out toward the horizon with a sleepy expression on his face while sipping from a drink. I bit my lip, debating with myself whether I ought to ask him about last night. In the end, I couldn't help but wander over.

He looked up as I approached… and smiled, no longer the grump he'd been yesterday. He also showed no signs of sobbing or falling into such a state of fear during the night, except for some crust in his inner eyes.

"You all right, Hazel?" he asked.

"Yeah," I said, clenching my jaw. "I, uh, I woke up last night and noticed you talking to yourself." I didn't want to embarrass him with the fact that I'd witnessed him sobbing, so this was the gentlest thing I could say.

He smirked. "Oh, really? What was I saying?"

"Uh, talking about how you didn't want someone, or something, to 'come again'… It was pretty creepy actually. I figured you must have been having a bad dream."

Peter's brows rose. "Weird," he muttered, taking another sip from his drink. "I don't remember a thing."

I stood eyeing him a moment longer, wondering if he was really telling the truth. I didn't detect embarrassment in his eyes, or dishonesty, so I guessed that he was.

I made an excuse to get away and headed back to

my group.

"Did you ask him?" Benedict asked, as he combed his hair.

"Said he didn't remember anything," I said.

"Probably was nothing then," Julian said. "Not sure why you even bothered asking."

I dropped the subject after that. We were soon made busy, anyway. We had to go hiking up the mountain to forage for water. We located a number of streams with crystal-clear water and filled up all our containers before returning to the beach for breakfast.

Although I had been trying to forget about the events of last night, I couldn't shake an uneasy feeling in my stomach. It hadn't just been that weird nightmare Peter had. It was the odd behavior portrayed by three of the guides so far—Gillian, Peter and Suzanne. Jamie and Charlie still seemed to be normal, but I couldn't help but find myself wondering when they would do an about face too.

As we swallowed down breakfast—more soup, like

last night (it would be soup for lunch and dinner too, since we'd run out of other fresh foods like sandwiches)—I asked Peter in a casual tone, "I guess the guides must have brought phones with them, right? Even if the rest of us left them behind…"

"Not phones, exactly," Peter replied. "We have walkie-talkie type things that are hooked up to the main island. That's how we'll call for the boat when it's time to leave."

"I see," I said, my stomach churning a little.

In that moment, I felt like I wanted to check in on my parents—to see how they were doing, and tell them about the erratic behavior of our guides. See what they thought of it all. For all I knew, Scottish people could just be the moody type. It would just be good to hear my mother's voice.

I stood up after finishing my soup and began wandering around the rest of our group, asking people whether they'd brought phones with them or not. All claimed they hadn't. To my disappointment, everyone had apparently surrendered to the

Murkbeech "adventure spirit". Even Wes couldn't help me out. So I had no choice but to give up the endeavor. If I started feeling even more uncomfortable, the urge to speak to my parents intensifying, I could always request to be taken back to the main island. I could even make up an excuse that I was feeling sick—which I actually was, kind of, with my headache—to make my request seem less flippant.

After breakfast, we ventured deeper into the island where our guides began a sort of botany class. Peter was back to his vibrant self, though Gillian appeared to have caught the moods again, and Suzanne was still rather prickly in her demeanor, just like last night. I stuck near Charlie, Jamie and Peter as they demonstrated how to apply dock leaf to a nettle rash, as well as showing us various other plants that could be used for food. They also taught us which plants to avoid, as well as teaching how to spot similar traits in families of plants. I wasn't sure how useful any of this would be outside Scotland or other parts of the

United Kingdom, but I found it all surprisingly interesting. So interesting that I almost forgot about last night, and the headache that persisted.

For lunch, we gathered a bunch of plants we had been shown along the way and roasted them over a fire along with some seaweed. After adding a sprinkle of salt, they were surprisingly delicious.

"Hey," said Wes, who had seated himself next to me. He had been holding a stick of skewered seaweed over the flames. "Want to try one of mine? They look better roasted than yours."

"Thanks," I said, wondering when I was going to stop blushing whenever he spoke to me. He handed me the entire skewer, obviously intending me to just bite off one of the chunks. I held it, waiting for it to cool down. Then, as I was about to take a bite, something hard rammed into me from behind. It felt like someone's knee. It sent me jerking forward and I almost pierced the back of my mouth with the sharp stick.

I choked, the skewer falling onto the sand, and

whirled around. I found myself gazing up at one of the four girls who shared Ruby's and my dormitory—the brunette who seemed to have taken a particular liking to Wes. She was just standing there, barely a foot away, staring down at me with darkened eyes.

"Excuse me?" I said, glaring at her incredulously. "What was that for?"

Wes also looked shocked as he stared at her.

"What was what for?" she asked, her voice infuriatingly calm. She planted her hands on her hips.

"You just knocked into me!"

She cocked her head to one side as she maintained steady eye contact. "Did I?" she wondered.

Where the heck is this girl coming from?

"Yes," Wes said, taking over from me. There was a heat to his voice as he picked up the ruined skewer of seaweed from the ground. "This could have stabbed Hazel's throat, you know."

"Oh, I'm sorry," she said, even though she

sounded everything but. "It was a complete accident."

I found myself at a loss for how to respond. I just gaped at her, disbelieving, until she turned around and walked away.

My eyes returned to Wes's. His confusion mirrored my own.

"What a harpy," Ruby said, who had witnessed what had happened too.

Yeah. That was a *really* bitchy thing to do. Those four girls had seemed uptight from the start, and likely the jealous sort, but what she'd just done… that seemed out of character even for her.

Out of character.

Like our guides.

"Are you okay?" Wes asked.

"Yeah," I managed. His skewer of roast seaweed was thoroughly ruined by now. He'd have to start again.

I glanced at Ruby, Julian and Benedict, before addressing Wes. "I'll, uh, see you in a bit."

I stood up, and the other three followed my cue to leave the circle around the fire where everyone was eating.

I looked seriously at each of them. "I think we should ask to be taken back to the main island," I said. "I want to call my parents."

"I don't think we are due to return for at least four days," Ruby said. "What excuse will you give?"

"I'll say I have a bad headache. Which isn't even a total lie."

There was a pause as they thought on it.

"Okay," Ruby said. "I agree."

"I agree too," Julian said.

Benedict nodded at me with his approval.

"It may be that I'm just being paranoid," I said, glancing back toward the fire. "That I'm seeing things that aren't there…" *That there's nothing supernatural involved here.* "But there's no harm in getting their opinion. Julian and Ruby could call their parents too. I'm sure they'd all appreciate a call in any case."

My eyes trained on Peter, I walked to him and sat down next to where he was eating on the sand.

"All right, Hazel?" he asked.

"Um, not really," I said, raising a hand to my forehead and rubbing it. "I've got a pretty bad headache. So have Ruby, Benedict and Julian. I think it's because we slept so close to the cave's entrance last night. We'd like to return to the hostel."

Peter frowned, examining my face. "May I feel your temperature?"

I nodded, though I wasn't sure if I actually had a temperature. It felt like just a headache.

He pressed his palm against my forehead and tutted. "Hm. You do feel a bit on the warm side actually. Come with me." He stood up and led me to the cave, where he stopped in front of his bag. He dove into one of its pockets and retrieved a dark green tube. "This is a natural plant-based remedy that works wonders for headaches," he said. "Hold out your palm."

Reluctantly, I extended my hand. He squeezed out

a blob of green paste into the center of my palm and instructed me to rub it against my temples. I did so and felt a slight tingling over my skin. He called the others over and had them do the same as me. "Now, give it twenty-four hours. If you still feel horrid, we'll take you back. Does that sound reasonable?"

I supposed it did. "Okay," I said.

Whether or not his balm did end up solving the headache, I'd have to tell him that it didn't tomorrow and that we needed to return. For now, I supposed, all we could do was wait.

Chapter 8: Hazel

I stuck with Julian, Ruby and Benedict for the rest of the day, avoiding everyone else except for Wes. We continued our scavenger training, which led us across the island as the guides showed all the things that were available to eat and those things that should be avoided.

We then came across a wide mud pit, and were encouraged to leap inside and… muck around. Since this whole trip was supposed to be about pushing your comfort zone, as much as I winced at the thought of getting all that grime in my hair, I was a good sport and entered along with everyone else—including my three comrades. We all stripped to our swimsuits and dove inside, where mud wars ensued. Some of our fellow "adventurers" ended up getting carried away, and a few boys got violent with each other—I was quite taken aback by their aggression. It caused the guides to put an end to the mud fight, which actually came as a disappointment to me.

The mud was unexpectedly pleasant, actually. It was thick and cool, which helped soothe my headache (which still wasn't showing signs of diminishing).

After climbing out of the pit, we headed to the lake to wash ourselves off and go for a swim.

These activities—in between meals and gathering some more water—took up the rest of the day. We had to leave the lake in good time in order to arrive back at the cave before dark.

"Still have a headache?" I mumbled to Ruby, who walked by my side.

"Yes," she said. "If anything the sun has made it

worse."

"Me too."

Peter's paste hadn't made the slightest bit of difference.

We had to gather more wood as soon as we reached base, and light a fire for the night. As the guides prepared some dinner, Wes took his usual seat beside me, his friend on the other side of Ruby. He let out a low groan before lying back and stretching his legs and arms. Then he sat up again.

"Doing okay?" he asked.

"Yeah."

I looked toward the four girls who sat opposite us. Usually they would be chatting, but now they sat still, just staring into the flames. Listlessly almost.

After we'd all been fed, Charlie told us another ghost story—about a man who, almost a hundred years ago, had been hanged for a crime somebody else had committed. Charlie said that his ghost was sometimes seen haunting the clifftops, which made me reluctant to look up at the one above us while it was dark.

Then it was time to turn in. The day had been tiring, and many were already starting to fall asleep while sitting around the fire. I suggested to Ruby, Benedict and Julian that we didn't sleep so close to the exit tonight, that we head toward the back of the cave, where the wind was less harsh. I didn't want our headaches to worsen overnight.

Most of the space at the back was taken, so we couldn't sleep all together in a row. We just had to set up in whatever small patch of ground was available and curl up in our sleeping bags.

I realized only as I had spread out my stuff to mark my territory how close I was to Wes. He smiled at me, then winked before he laid his head down for the night.

I let out a deep breath as I pulled my cover high over my chest, so that it covered my neck from the draft. And then, slowly, exhaustion coaxed me to sleep.

***

Just like the previous night, I woke with a start in the early hours of the morning. It wasn't to something as gentle as sobbing though. It was to the sound of people cussing, shouting, struggling.

I shot bolt upright and gaped around the cave toward the noise. To my shock, the four snotty girls (including the brunette) were on their feet near the entrance and attempting to hit each other with pots and pans they must have taken from the campsite. Another boy—who had arrived on the trip on his own—was also joining in the fight with a stick.

What is going on?

It felt like I had woken up in a dream.

"Stop it!" I shouted across the cave.

This roused others who had been drifting in semi-consciousness. I jumped up and rushed toward the brawl, almost tripping over Wes, who stumbled to his feet and staggered after me.

"Stop!" I called again.

The guides woke up, looking utterly bewildered.

The brawlers moved out of the cave, dropping down on the sand where they continued to fight.

Wes and I were among the first to approach. I dove for one girl, while Wes dove for the boy. I caught sight of the glint of a blade in the moonlight. The boy was holding a knife.

"No!" I screamed.

The boy's blade plunged into Wes's shoulder. He let out a deep groan before collapsing.

Peter flung himself at the boy and managed to disarm him, but it was too late. I dropped down to where Wes lay on the sand and stared down in horror at the stab wound. At least the knife hadn't driven into his gut, but it chilled me to think that boy might've been aiming for his throat, to have cut him so high on his body.

"We need to get back to the mainland!" I cried.

Thankfully, the guides agreed. Some of the stronger boys among Wes's group helped to restrain the girls involved in the fight, along with the boy who'd stabbed Wes, which freed Peter to hurry back to the cave. He rummaged for his "walkie-talkie" and made an emergency call to the island.

When he returned to us on the sand, he informed us that a boat would arrive as soon as possible—on this very beach—and that, until the guides got to the bottom of what on earth had just happened and why, we should all return to the hostel together.

Thank God.

Everyone shared the same expression as we hurried back to the cave to gather our things. Confusion, shock.

"Well, this trip went down Crazy Lane fast," Benedict murmured as we rolled up our sleeping bags and stuffed them into our backpacks.

Yeah. We probably would've been better off just staying in The Shade for our school break. Going away was overrated.

As soon as we packed up our things, I hurried back to Wes, who was being treated by Suzanne and Gillian. They had applied a compress over his shoulder and given him some kind of medication. His forehead was drenched with sweat, his face pale, eyes tightly closed.

I wanted to ask if he was all right, but he didn't look like he was in the mood to talk.

"What the hell has gotten into you?" Jamie yelled at the brawlers.

Bizarrely, they responded in much the same way as the brunette had the day before when she'd knocked me. They didn't really have anything to say for themselves—no semblance of an excuse or reason for why they had lashed out at each other.

"I just want to be back home now," I whispered to Ruby, Julian and my brother.

There was no way that this trip could be playing out anything like the way my parents had envisioned it.

Something was wrong with Murkbeech Adventures, both the islands and the people.

Relief washed over me as the boat arrived. Wes was carried on first by Jamie and Peter, and then the five culprits were escorted on after, so they could be kept near the back of the boat.

After we had all boarded, the captain propelled us

away from the island and back toward the company's private jetty on Murkbeech Island.

Wes looked like he was starting to drift in and out of consciousness. Two of his friends, who'd been thoughtful enough to pick up Wes's things for him, hovered over him.

"Hey, you all right, man?" one of them asked.

Wes didn't respond.

"You're going to be okay," Gillian assured him, once again switching to her compassionate, nurturing mood.

Though I couldn't ignore the way her hands were trembling. So were Suzanne's as they exchanged glances with their colleagues.

I hurried to the front of the boat and gazed ahead as the dark outline of Murkbeech loomed closer, as if by will alone I could make us travel faster.

Once we reached the jetty, everyone made way for Wes to be carried off first. Then the five violent teens were dragged off. Two buggy vehicles were waiting on the grass, one of which Wes was loaded into, the other reserved for the five offenders. As they sped away toward the hostel, I guessed that Wes would immediately be taken to the doctor's room (there was supposed to be an experienced one on site at all times due to the various risky activities kids got up to here) and as for the group of five, they'd likely be taken into isolation until their guardians came to collect them from the island, maybe even the police in the case of the boy who had stabbed Wes. There was no way that it had been an accident.

The rest of us were left to use our flashlights to trek our way through the darkness, back to the building.

As soon as we reached the hostel, we rushed to our dorms for our phones. I grabbed mine and was about to dial my parents' number when I realized there was no signal. There had been just a couple of days ago. Something had happened since we'd been on the other island.

"Ruby, do you have a signal?" I asked, my heartbeat quickening.

"No," she said hoarsely.

Crap.

We raced out of the dorm and into the boys' area. We found Julian and Benedict standing in the hallway, holding their phones at various angles, trying to get a signal.

"Dammit," Ruby hissed.

What is going on?

"There's got to be a rational explanation," Julian said, although he didn't speak with much conviction.

"Let's try outside," I suggested.

We ran to the main entrance and, holding our phones high above our heads, zigzagged across the gravel parking lot, willing our phones to pick up on a signal. Then we hurried to the nearest hillock and climbed to the top. Still no luck.

"Okay," I said, trying to keep my calm. "We'll ask Peter or someone to take us back to the mainland. There we'll find a signal, or a phone booth if worst comes to worst."

We sprinted back to the hostel. We were about to

go bursting into the sitting room where a map of the facility hung when we caught sight of another fight that had broken out further down the hallway. This was a fight among boys. Wes's friends.

Then we heard shouting to our left. Our attention switched to the opposite hallway where another fight had broken out among a group of seven girls.

What. The. Heck.

I still hadn't wrapped my mind around what was happening.

What went wrong? This trip started out like a romance novel.

I hated unexpected switches of genre within books, and much more in real life. My headache felt like it was intensifying from the stress, my forehead feeling close to splitting from the pain.

No longer able to stifle our panic, we hurried into the sitting room, which was empty. We approached the map that hung above the mantelpiece and scanned it. The staff residences were located at the back of the building, behind the kitchens.

We crossed the living room and entered the adjoining dining room. We barged through the door behind the canteen and emerged in the kitchen. We pushed through another door at the back of it, which led us through to another corridor lined with twelve doors—the staff's apartments.

We knocked loudly on each door and yelled for help. Nobody answered. We even tried to open the doors, but they were locked.

"They're probably all in the doctor's building with Wes," Julian said.

Yes, yes. That would make sense.

We pushed through the fire exit at the end of the hallway and stumbled out into the cool night. The horse stables were directly ahead of us, and to our right was a small brick building hidden from view from the front of the hostel. Small solar-powered lights dug into the grass led the way to the building.

Running along the sidewalk that lined the back wall of the main hostel, we were about to launch onto the grass path when we witnessed yet another fight going on to our right. Outside, in the cold open air.

Ruby swore.

This fight was hard to ignore. There were almost ten teens involved—a mixture of girls and boys throwing punches and kicks and head-butting each other. It was getting bloody fast.

"Stop it!" I roared, my panic channeling into aggression. "STOP BEHAVING LIKE ANIMALS!"

Five of them stopped fighting and turned on us, their faces contorted with anger.

Yelling to them had been a mistake.

I hadn't thought that this night could get any worse, but the next thing I knew, the entire mob was lurching toward us, their hands balled into fists.

Oh, man.

We galloped across the field toward the doctor's building, slamming up against its front door as we reached it. I gripped the handle and yanked it down to find that—to my sheer relief—it wasn't locked. I flung it open and pulled Ruby, Benedict and Julian inside before I hauled it shut. The door vibrated with the force of our pursuers crashing against it. They began grasping at the handle. Ruby spotted a bolt and pulled it. Still, I didn't feel comfortable leaving it unguarded.

Julian seemed to be reading my thoughts. "I'll stay here," he said.

"I will too," Ruby said.

"What about the windows?" Benedict croaked.

"Search this floor for windows and make sure they're all shut," I told him.

I wasn't sure if whatever madness had possessed them would cause them to actually start smashing the windows.

In the meantime, I had to get help from the grownups.

To our left was an open doorway leading into a dark sitting room, which Benedict hurried into, while I hurried to the door directly in front of me. A sign displaying the name "Doctor Murdock" hung from it. There was no time to knock. I pushed it open and found myself in a room with thankfully sane-looking people.

Wes was lying on a treatment bed in the center of a sterile medical room; about ten of the island's staff gathered around him worriedly—including Peter.

"Peter!" I gasped, approaching the edge of the bed. "People have gone… crazy!" I wasn't even sure how to describe the situation, it was so bizarre. "They're fighting each other!"

"What?" Peter asked. "Who?"

"Everyone!" I panted, clutching my throbbing head. "They've become like animals. All hell's broken loose in the dorms, and outside. I don't know what's gotten—"

I stopped short as the expression of every single adult in the room suddenly distorted. Their faces went from alarmed to disdainful and irritated within the space of three seconds.

Even Wes, who'd been lying on his back, abruptly sat up and glared at me.

I already knew that I had to run. Run where, I had

no idea. But I had to get out of this room.

I backed away and slipped out of the door before slamming it shut behind me. Julian and Ruby, who were still manning the increasingly vibrating door, looked at me with utter terror. It seemed they'd already guessed what was happening from the look on my face.

"The adults have switched too!" I breathed. "And Wes!"

Ruby and Julian gasped, while Benedict came hurrying to us from the sitting room. "The windows are all clo…" He froze as he stared at the closed door behind me, which was also beginning to thunder from slamming fists, the door handle rattling.

We were trapped. Completely and utterly screwed. I couldn't think of a single way out of this situation without having to face either the mob behind me or the mob in front of me.

It was a matter of deciding which was worse.

My mind was still jammed with fear as I replayed the way Wes had suddenly sat up, as though he'd entered a state of consciousness so consuming he was no longer even aware of his physical ailment.

He might even be standing now, and be one of the people trying to open the door.

Benedict helped me keep it shut, but we were losing this game. Fast.

"What do we do?" my brother wheezed.

I glanced toward the sitting room. I could think of no option other than to let go of the doors, dart as deep into the house as possible, try to climb through a window and run away from the building... run where, I had no freaking clue.

But we didn't even get a chance to attempt that harebrained scheme as the pressure behind Benedict and me became too strong. We didn't have a bolt helping us, like Ruby and Julian.

My brother and I found ourselves hurtling forward as the door jerked forward. We stumbled and tripped, and then the adults were upon us. Hands closed around the back of my neck and around my arms and legs.

I was flipped over onto my back, and that was when I realized that Wes was among the aggressors. He had latched on to my right wrist.

"What the HELL!" Benedict spluttered in indignation as he was wrestled into submission along with our other two companions. "Let GO of me!"

I had been expecting them to start behaving in the same way as the teens outside, with aggression. Punching us. Beating us. But their objective, for whatever strange reason, appeared to be different. They were making us submit, and then they were dragging us toward the front door. I kicked and flailed in their grasp, but as a human, I was no match for three grown men. Not even my coursing adrenaline could save me.

The bolt was drawn. The night air spilled into the entrance room. And then we were hauled outside.

I expected us to be battered by the teens who'd lost their minds outside the house. But, to my bewilderment, they had calmed down, turned on their heel, and were now all heading back to the hostel.

"What are you doing?" Julian yelled.

None of our captors answered as they continued dragging us across the lawn.

Then Ruby gasped to my right. As I strained to look in the direction we were headed, I realized why.

Five imposing figures were sweeping toward us in the darkness. They were men, the tallest I'd ever seen—each must've been over six and a half feet tall. They couldn't be human. They wore long, sweeping black cloaks, and as they ventured closer, within the halo of light emanating from the solar bulbs, I was able to better make out their features.

Each was pale and shared the same harsh jawline. Perhaps they were brothers. One in particular caught my eye; the tallest among them, he was staring right at me. He had straight, russet-brown hair that trailed past his shoulders and his eyes were raven black.

Our captors dropped us abruptly onto the grass. I scrambled to stand up along with Ruby, Julian and Benedict, but was immediately overcome by dizziness. The pain in my head had reached a whole new level of agony as the five tall men approached.

Before we could even attempt to run, the men sped up. One lurched straight for Ruby, one for Julian, one for Benedict and two for me, including the tallest.

They darted forward with supernatural speed, the tallest reaching me before the other. He stopped three feet away from me before sliding a hand beneath his cloak and whipping out a long, razor-sharp sword, which he brandished against the second man.

"No, Jenus," the tall man said. His voice was deep and fierce, like the bark of a wild dog. "You must stay within this realm and find another. This one shall be mine."

An angry scowl contorted Jenus' face as he backed away. When the tall man turned and stared down at me with his intense black eyes, the combination of shock and my splitting migraine overpowered me. As he stooped down to wrap his powerful arms around me and pick me up, I passed out.

Chapter 9: Hazel

My brain became aware of an ache at the back of my jaw. I was clenching my teeth hard. I loosened my jaw as I sensed light behind my eyelids. Then the sound of crackling. Soothing warmth touched my skin and I was lying face down on my stomach, on something soft and smooth.

Forcing my eyes open, I found myself bathed in firelight. Beneath me was a feathery rug, and in front of me was a giant fireplace, flames rising up high and licking its charred walls.

I propped myself upright, my vision focusing. I

was in a small room whose towering walls were made of wide stone slabs, and whose floors were populated with an antique-looking chaise longue, a wooden chair padded with silk cushioning, and a narrow wooden table on the opposite side of the room.

My breathing loud in my ears, I staggered to my feet. I was still trying to work out where I was and how I'd gotten here. What had happened? What was my last memory?

Then it all came flooding back. The nightmare of Murkbeech. Those five tall men, leaping at us. One of them stooping down to pick me up.

After that, all went dark.

Oh, God. What were those things? Why do they want us?

Where am I now?

I realized that I didn't have a headache anymore. That was a small mercy at least.

My eyes darted around me and rested on a tall, rounded door. I hurried to it and clutched its ancient iron handle. I thrust downward, but it wouldn't budge. My heart in my throat, I ran to the other side of the room, where there appeared to be a shuttered window. Prying my hands into the ruts of the black wooden shutter, I pulled hard until it creaked and swung open.

I was met with a blast of ice-cold air, and then a sight so awe-inspiring and terrifying that I struggled to breathe for several moments.

Whether it was dusk or dawn was hard to tell, but bathed in a misty hue of pale orange sunlight was some kind of city, or country, sprawled out beneath me for as far as I could see. I was standing in a room near the top of a gargantuan dark gray stone castle, perched atop a rolling hill and guarded all around by high walls and a wide, treacherous-looking moat.

The civilization on the other side of the walls and water looked like it belonged in some kind of medieval-fantasy video game. Broad stone buildings as dark as the castle clustered the landscape amidst cobbled stone roads and paths. Many constructions had chimneys which billowed thick smoke, adding to the haze that hung over the community.

A harsh cawing called my attention to my right. Within the boundaries of the castle was a spacious courtyard, in the corner of which were five massive birds with sharp beaks and long heads. They looked like vultures, but no vultures you'd find on Earth. These looked capable of carrying three full-grown men.

I began to wheeze in panic.

Where did they bring us?

I'd heard many tales from my family about places in the supernatural realm, but none fit the description of this sinister-looking place. It had the dark vibe I'd pictured Cruor having, except this was inhabited… by whom, I still didn't understand.

A powerful gust of wind rattled the shutter and warded me back inside.

Fear climbing in my chest, I moved back to the door with balled fists. Even though I was terrified to attract the attention of my captor, I had to know what was going on. I had to know that my brother and Ruby and Julian were still safe. *Still alive.*

I smashed my fists against the door and called out, "Let me out of here!". I shuddered to imagine what might be on the other side.

I continued banging as loud as I could until I heard the first echoes of footsteps approaching. Then I stopped. I withdrew from the door, my hands beginning to tremble. The footsteps drew closer and closer until they stopped, right outside the door. Then came the scraping of a key against metal… and the door creaked open.

I staggered backward, the back of my legs hitting against the chaise longue. The door creaked wide open, revealing a breathtakingly tall man, standing in the doorway, his hair tied at the back of his head. It was the same man who'd grabbed me. Without his long cloak, he wore dark pants and a loose black shirt that flashed a portion of toned chest. He wasn't as bulky as I had imagined. He was well built, but still slim and lithe. I was so consumed by the intensity of his dark eyes as they settled on me that it took me a few seconds to register that he hadn't arrived alone. Perched on his left shoulder was some kind of cat. It looked like a lynx. Its ears were pointed, and it had a warm brown coat criss-crossed with black streaks. Its eyes were slanted and yellowish.

"A-Are you a warlock?" I demanded of the man, my gaze shooting back to him.

His harsh mouth twitched slightly upward in one corner, forming a fleeting smirk.

"No," he replied. His voice stirred the room like a sonorous drum.

He stepped inside and shut the door sharply behind him. As he strode to the cushioned chair, he moved with fluid intent, with grace and swiftness that only a supernatural could possess. He sat down and the lynx leapt from his shoulder to the floor, where it stood upright by the man's large booted feet.

"Then what are you?" I breathed. He didn't strike me as a vampire. Although he was pale, he wasn't pale enough. And besides, it didn't look like he had fangs. Plus, how would being a vampire explain the craziness that had gone on at Murkbeech?

He crossed his arms and kept me hanging for ten seconds as he continued to study my face. Finally he replied, "That would depend on who you ask… The son of an emperor. A hated rival. The most feared swordsman in all of Nevertide… This I am known as and more. But I suppose what you wish to know is my name—Tejus Hellswan—and that I am a sentry."

My mouth hung open as I gaped at him.

Nevertide?

Sentry?

"Wh-What is a sentry?" I managed, sinking down to the chaise-longue for fear that my knees were becoming too weak to hold me.

"Some call us mindguards, masters of thought control, leeches of emotion… Though in some ways we are not so very different from humans. We are of flesh and blood. But unlike humans, we possess heightened strength and speed, and our stamina is not derived from the food we put in our stomachs.

We sustain our powers by feeding off mental energy... much like vampires feed off blood, I suppose."

Sentries. Whoa. I wondered if anyone in The Shade was aware of their existence. I doubted it. I'd never once heard mention of them.

"Wh-What were you doing on Earth? And what have you done with my brother and two friends?"

He pried his focus away from me and roamed slowly to the window I had left open. His lynx followed him, though it cast its gaze back at me while they walked.

Tejus stopped at the window and, placing his hands on the window frame, gazed out at the view.

"Come," he commanded me, not turning around.

I didn't think that it was a good idea to disobey this guy—at least not yet, not until I'd figured out what the heck was going on and just how bad my situation was—so I rose to my feet and cautiously made my way over to the window. But I found it surprisingly difficult to approach within a few feet of him. It was as if the two of us were opposing magnets, as though a halo of intense energy surrounded him, making me recoil.

He turned at my hesitation. I'd expected there to be an irritable look on his face, but instead his handsome features were formed in a thoughtful expression.

"I was right about the strength of your mind," he said quietly.

My brows lowered. *"What?"*

"My brothers and I descended to the human realm because we were each in search of a cohort. We have a grave task ahead of us, and we require an aide whose mind is both sturdy and fertile to provide us with strength throughout whatever trials we might come across."

"Task? Trials? *What* are you talking about?"

"Come closer." He beckoned me again.

I flinched at the thought. I'd backed away, afraid that my migraine would come on again. "I-It's hard."

"I've relinquished my mind's energy. It won't be

so difficult to approach. Come, stand by me."

Inhaling, I attempted to move forward again. This time, as he promised, it wasn't difficult. There was no weird forcefield around him prodding me backward.

I stood beside him at the window, even as the gale-force wind swept back my hair and caused my skin to break out in goosebumps.

Standing two feet away from me, he raised a hand and pointed deep into the horizon. "Look beyond the Hellswan Kingdom, far into the distance. Do you see the outline of a second kingdom? The wall that surrounds it?"

I squinted. It was so hard to see through the haze, especially now that the sun seemed to be setting—it was dusk after all. But after a few seconds, yes, I realized what he was talking about. I could see the faintest trace of a high wall.

I nodded.

"That is a second kingdom within the land of Nevertide. Ruled by King Dellian Demzred. It is just as large as ours, with just as many worthy knights and foot soldiers… Now look eastward." He pointed to our left. "You will not be able to see it at this time of day with your poor human eyesight, but therein lies a third kingdom of Nevertide—or rather, queendom—ruled by Queen Trina Seraq. There are still more kingdoms—three more, to be precise—that make up the six provinces of Nevertide. Six provinces managed by five kings and one queen, but ruled over by a single emperor, to ensure consistent harmony in our land… That emperor is my father."

This was really a lot of information to absorb in such a short space of time. I found my head spinning.

"So your father is Emperor of Nevertide… which makes you a prince?"

Tejus nodded. "One of five princes," he replied.

"Where is Nevertide?" I asked, my eyes sweeping the seemingly never-ending landscape. I wasn't exactly a geographer of the supernatural dimension, but it would be helpful to know where we were near at least.

"That I cannot tell you," Tejus said, backing away from the window with his feline and retaking his seat in the chair.

I stayed by the window and turned to look at him. "Why not?" I shot back.

"It is sentry law to keep our whereabouts secret. Very few know how to find our land, and it's unlikely that you would find it marked on any map. Not even the witches of The Sanctuary know where we live… But I have not finished answering your initial questions," he said, raising a dark brow.

"So tell me what you mean by tasks and trials."

His lynx purred deeply, nestling the side of its head against Tejus' ankles as it continued to watch me.

"I told you that my father is Emperor of Nevertide," he said, "but he will not be for long. He will soon have used up the duration of rule—many thousands of moons have passed since he was coronated—and very soon, a new emperor must be appointed. And it must be the most worthy man or woman in the empire."

His reply did little to provide clarity to my situation. I couldn't deny that I was curious to know more about this surreal world, but right now my mind could only focus on what was directly relevant to myself and my companions getting out of here.

"Where did you put my brother and two friends?" I demanded more loudly than I had before. "Take me to them!"

I was of half a mind to run to the door and try to open it again—even though that was a ludicrous proposition since there was no way I could run from him, and even if I could, where would I run?—when Tejus replied, "Your human companions are not under my wing. They were taken by my brothers, as you saw, and will serve as cohorts for the task ahead."

Task. That word again.

"*WHAT TASK*?" The fear and desperation coursing through my veins felt like they were bringing me close to a nervous breakdown.

Tejus remained calm, his expression controlled. I

got the sense with him that every action he took was deliberate and calculated, whether he was talking or walking across the room. If he had the power to control the minds of others, I guessed it was only logical to assume that he must have the ability to control his own mind too.

"You must learn to harness your emotions," he remarked.

I felt like cursing him. "Harnessing my emotions would be a lot easier if you would take me to my brother and friends," I snapped.

"Sit down," he said, gesturing to the chaise-longue. Only a few minutes ago he'd been beckoning me to the window. I didn't feel like sitting down—least of all at his command—so I remained standing, crossing my arms over my chest.

A few seconds later, I instantly wished I'd obeyed his request. I felt a searing pain in my skull—the migraine had returned.

"Ugh!" I huffed, rushing to the chaise longue and dropping down onto it. "Okay," I seethed. "I'm sitting." Even as Tejus' dark eyes continued to hold me, the headache gradually diminished, allowing me to see and think clearly again. "What did you do to me? And to all those other humans back in Murkbeech? Why did you make them all go insane?"

"We were conducting a test," Tejus explained. "A test to discover humans whose minds we could not easily crack... We had visited that small island before—some months ago in human time. We found only adults there, whose minds were disappointingly weak. We were able to manipulate their desires and emotions to doing our bidding very quickly, and thus they were not worthy cohorts for us."

The adults. I wondered what the sentries' mind control had involved exactly—whether it caused those adults to be permanently damaged, and that was why they had behaved so erratically around us. Switching from one mood to the other for no apparent reason at the drop of a hat.

Then there was the matter of Peter's nightmare... His pleading in his sleep for something to not return.

"Why did you return?" I couldn't help but ask.

"We had moved on to other places within the human realm in search of suitable minds, but our task was proving to be far more difficult than any of us had expected. It is rare to find a human mind that is sturdy enough to take a sentry's pressure, you see… And after infiltrating a person's mind, we never truly leave," he said. "We are able to tap in from time to time, and we discovered by this process that a large group of humans—young humans—were soon to arrive on the island. Since we hadn't had luck recruiting cohorts elsewhere, we decided to return and try our luck… and indeed, we were very lucky. We began testing out the young people, slowly and subtly at first, testing the waters—we discovered very quickly that most were just as weak-minded as any other human we'd come across so far… But then when we tested you and your three friends, we discovered something we'd been searching for all along. Minds that were strong, healthy and self-assured enough to not break under pressure—exactly what we required."

So my headache… The migraines we'd experienced had not been due to the fact we'd been sleeping near the entrance of the cave. It had been these sentry creatures trying to mess with our minds all along.

"You're saying you can't crack our minds to control us at all?" I asked, a surge of nervousness rushing through me. These creatures might not have fangs or claws, but they were dangerous in a different and more pernicious way.

Tejus' lips curved in a half-smile. "I never said that," he replied. "There are very few minds we cannot crack… What I said was that your minds were—and are—hardy. They will not break at the first, second, or even third touch. Which allows us to feed off your mental energy without breaking you."

These creatures truly did sound like vampires. "Feed off our mental energy," I repeated. "What does that even mean?"

The lynx leapt off Tejus' lap as he rose to his feet again. My heartbeat quickened as he strode toward me, stopping just three feet in front of me.

Then I felt it—that same intense forcefield manifest around him. That strange, magnetic energy. I wanted to stand up and get as far away from him as I could in the room. But I couldn't stand up without moving at least a little bit closer, which I found myself barely able to do. I felt repelled by his energy, and yet it wasn't repelled by me. It was attempting to suck me in… or suck at me. Absorb me, almost. *God, this is strange.* I felt an odd feeling of pressure around my ears, my brain feeling bloated and light.

And then it stopped, just as abruptly as it had started.

I realized only as he stepped backward that I had been holding my breath the whole time. I expected to perhaps feel a headache again, but I didn't.

"That's what it feels like," Tejus explained, as if he'd read my thoughts. "I'm sure you will have noticed the difference between the times I begin an attempt to break into your mind, and the times I merely absorb some of your energy."

The former involved a migraine, while the latter involved… I wasn't even sure how to describe it.

"S-So if you actually broke into our minds—went all the way—we'd become brain-damaged for life like those adults you messed with?"

He shook his head. "Not immediately. At least not immediately in your and your friends' case, because you have a stronger resistance. Everyone's strength is different though, so for some it only takes one visit by us into their minds to become damaged, others two, three, or four times."

"So you just go around meddling with innocent humans and potentially ruining the rest of their lives!" I said, looking at him with disgust.

He remained stoic, and chose not to comment.

"WHAT is so special about us anyway?" I asked the question that had been nagging me since the beginning of our conversation.

Now a hint of amusement crossed his face again. "Only you could tell me that," he said. "I have not broken into your mind… yet."

I swallowed. The only thing that set Benedict, Ruby, Julian and me apart from the rest of Murkbeech's residents was that we were from The Shade. "Shadians". Could the fact that we had come from such an unconventional background compared to other humans make our minds stronger, more independent? Or was it something to do with growing up so close to supernaturals?

I could only guess. But wondering about the ifs, ands, or buts wasn't bringing me any closer to locating my brother and friends.

I was glad when Tejus resumed the conversation before I could prompt him again.

"So my brothers and I discovered you and your three companions, and each claimed one of you. My fifth brother remains in the human dimension, where he will have to continue looking for a worthy cohort… If he doesn't find a suitable one in time then, well, he will be at a disadvantage to the rest of us. We can feed off other supernaturals' energy—even Nevertide's animals"—he bent down to his lynx and scratched its ear as he continued—"but none are quite so potent as humans."

"Maybe you will finally be so kind as to tell me what this test actually is now," I said through gritted teeth.

"As I mentioned, my father will soon reach the end of his emperorship, and a new emperor will be chosen for Nevertide—by the next eclipse, in a few dozen moons from now. He or she shall be chosen from the existing kings and queen of Nevertide's provinces. In order to allow Hellswan Kingdom to gain another chance at being the ruling province, my father will also step down as king—giving way to the most worthy and capable sentry in all of Hellswan Kingdom."

"And you are the eldest son?" I asked him, frowning.

"Indeed, I am," he replied, his irises shimmering darkly.

"So then you would be your father's natural choice? You would be put forward?"

"Not necessarily," he said. "I might be his eldest son but I do not get immediate preference for his crown. Nor do any of my brothers. The net will be cast far and wide across all of Hellswan Kingdom—and any man or woman of eligible age is beckoned to compete for rulership in a perilous contest."

My breath hitched. This was getting worrisome fast. Was he expecting me, my brother, Julian and Ruby to get roped into all of this? It sounded risky and dangerous. What kind of tests would a person be put to in a competition for the crown of Nevertide's emperor? Something told me that it would be anything but easy.

Before I could express anything, however, Tejus ploughed on. "There are some rules to this contest, however. Each family within Hellswan Kingdom can only put forward one representative at once. No siblings can enter; the heads of the families must think long and hard and choose whom among siblings is most worthy to represent them… and likely to succeed."

I wrinkled my nose in confusion. "Then why are you and your brothers—?"

Tejus smiled grimly. "Being sons of a king, and the current Emperor of Nevertide no less, we have some… extra hoops to jump through. My father wants to be sure that he is truly putting forward the very best man to represent the Hellswan family—he cannot merely assume that I fit that role without putting us all through a test… and it is this test that you will help us with first."

"What does the test involve?" I asked, finding it gradually more difficult to breathe.

"We do not know exactly—if we did, it would not be much of a test. All we know is that it involves a labyrinth and a sword located right in the middle which we must all work to claim. The first to reach the sword shall be put forward to represent the Hellswan family in the battle to compete for the right to Hellswan Kingdom's throne, and then, potentially, fight for emperorship."

This all sounded very stressful. *Certainly not how I*

was intending to spend my summer vacation.

My mouth had dried out completely by now. "So you kidnapped us to... *come with you* during this contest with your brothers? And what about the brother who emerges victorious? What then?"

"Yes, we took each of you to assist us and keep our minds sharp, our physical strength as strong as it can possibly be during the labyrinth quest... and after that, whichever of us emerges victorious and attains the right to compete for Hellswan's throne, our human will be required to come with us to the next step too—winning our kingdom's throne and keeping our family's royal status."

Even though there was still a mountain of things I didn't understand about Tejus, this sinister land, and my supposed role in it, I'd gotten enough of an answer by now to understand where this was going. And I would have no part in it. None of us could.

Heat rose in my cheeks as indignation surged in my chest. These sentries' mindset was everything The Shade had worked to change—that humans only existed to be of use to more powerful supernaturals. The past two years of GASP's activities had worked to stamp out this attitude from every corner, and fought to create a world of mutual respect and cooperation between supernaturals. I was going to give this arrogant, conceited "prince" a piece of my mind… so to speak.

"I am not your plaything!" I stormed. "And neither are my human companions. You cannot simply kidnap us and expect us to go along with whatever selfish plans you have! I have a family back home!" *A family who will soon be freaking out over our unexplained disappearance.* "A mother! A father! Uncles, aunts, cousins. And my brother is only fourteen years old, do you know that?" I became so enraged as I spoke that I found myself leaping to my feet and stalking toward him, even though his size terrified me—it was as if I'd become immune to it. "Imagine if you were stripped from your mother as a boy. Would you have liked that?" I was standing but two feet from him now, hands on my hips, glaring into his dark eyes. They had been completely unwavering in their steady gaze back at me, but although he remained calm, as I mentioned his mother, he averted his gaze.

"I do not have a mother," he replied, his voice cold.

I inhaled. *Trust me to pick the wrong example.* Although I didn't wish growing up without a mother on anyone, I couldn't exactly bring myself to feel sorry for this guy right now, considering that he was treating us like slaves.

"Well, a father then," I said irritably. "You get the point…" I wanted to threaten him that I was a *Novak*, and bring home the significance of it—that pissing off my parents and grandparents was a *very* bad idea. But I didn't know if these creatures knew about The Shade, and I felt hesitant to mention it, considering that I still knew so little about them as a species. I didn't know how effective witches were on them, whether sentries might even be able to use their powers to crack a witch's mind through a protective magic boundary. Considering that I'd never heard any of our witches speak of sentries before, it was possible that The Shade's witches didn't even know of their existence.

So I kept quiet about this aspect of my history for now. The last thing I wanted was to give these monsters any ideas and cause trouble for my home. If a Shadian's mind was indeed stronger than a regular human's, we had plenty of other humans on the island they could mess with if they got the chance... Their minds were also strong enough apparently to affect phone signals.

When my rant ended—Tejus still not looking directly at me—I felt his lynx snaking around my legs. Although it was unfair of me—it was just an animal—I felt irritated by it, like it was a representation of Tejus himself, and brushed it aside unceremoniously.

The lynx narrowed its piercing eyes on me and hissed, baring its fangs.

I felt like hissing back.

My chest was tense with anxiety at the thought of Benedict. My poor little brother. It killed me to think how terrified he must be right now. I had no idea how widely the personalities of these Hellswan brothers ranged. I prayed he wasn't being hurt… and would come out mentally intact after this.

"I understand your sentiments for your brother and friends," Tejus said, his voice low and throaty as he broke the span of silence and looked at me again. He stepped toward me, reminding me again just how imposing a man he was as he towered over me. I found myself backing away a bit more. "For this reason," he went on, "I have a proposal to make to you, Hazel… what is your second name?"

"Achilles," I grunted.

"Hazel Achilles."

It felt weird to hear him utter my name. I felt taken aback initially that he even knew my first name, considering he wasn't supposed to have broken into my mind yet. But I reminded myself that he and his brothers had been hanging around the

Scottish islands for a while before they'd made themselves known to us; they were the cause of all the initial strange happenings with those bitchy girls Ruby and I had shared a dorm with, as well as everyone else... including Wes. It was more than likely he'd heard my name being called by someone.

I scowled. I didn't want to negotiate or come to any kind of compromise. I just wanted to be reunited with Benedict, Ruby and Julian, and get out of here. "What *proposal*?" I asked.

"Each of you will accompany us during our first trial, the test set by our father, between us brothers. Then, *if* you cooperate with me to your full capacity, and I win the contest and gain the right to compete for the king's crown, I shall convince my father to order my brothers to free *your* brother and friends, and they shall be returned to the human realm... You, however, shall remain."

My breath hitched, my blood pounding in my ears. "What?"

His jaw stiffened, his gaze intensifying, and I

sensed that somewhere beneath his stiff exterior he was beginning to lose patience with me, and there was only so long he might continue tolerating my barrage of protest...

"You heard me. And this is the most generous proposal you will receive," he replied, clipped.

As much as I was frightened by the thought of all of us staying in this land for even another hour, I supposed that it was better than nothing. I didn't doubt Tejus when he said I would be receiving no more offers from him. After all, he technically hadn't even had to make his first offer; we were all stuck here, with no means of escape. Even when our parents found out that we were gone, where would they even begin to look if they had no clue that sentries even existed, much less the location of their land?

I guessed that Tejus had made this proposal only to make me cooperate. It would be hard for him to focus on his "task" if I was rebelling and fighting him at every turn. He needed to leech from my mind, for me to be a source of strength for him, rather than stress.

Tejus was smart—calculating, as I'd detected from the beginning.

If I managed to help him win against his brothers, and Tejus kept his word, then at least the other three could go home. My brother could be returned to safe hands. And they could tell our family everything about what they'd witnessed: the existence of sentries, and that I was still trapped here. They might not know where this realm was, but I didn't put it past them to figure out how to find it… maybe even set some sort of trap… It was annoying that I had been unconscious on the journey here. I hadn't been awake to witness whether or not Tejus had carried me through a portal in Nevertide itself, or borrowed some other land's portal before traveling here…

"When you arrived through the portal in Nevertide," I said abruptly, "had any of my companions passed out?"

A question with a hidden significance—I needed

him to comment on whether or not there was a portal leading here directly… but I should have known that Tejus was too sharp to fall for that trick.

"Whether there is a portal here or not," he replied, "is not something I plan to tell you."

I gulped. If there *was* a portal here in Nevertide, it would make the prospect of me being rescued far more hopeful. If my brother, Ruby and Julian made it home, The Shade would have to somehow discover where it was…

"And what if you don't succeed?" I asked Tejus. "What if one of your brothers does? Then what? I will have gone to the trouble of helping you for nothing."

"Correct," Tejus replied, his expression stony. "That is why you must do all you can to help me succeed. You and your three human companions would remain here forever… since I can assure you that none of my brothers will have bothered to make such a generous proposal as I have to you."

I exhaled sharply. This truly was sink or swim.

What about this first "trial" set by his father? Would it be perilous? I couldn't even bring myself to consider the contests that would follow that—should Tejus win, I would be dragged along with him… And what if a different sentry won? What if Benedict's captor did? Would Benedict be dragged along with him to the next level of competing for the role of king? Something told me that would be a lot more strenuous.

Ugh. There were so many layers of unknowns to this situation my nerves felt like they were fraying at the ends, my brain close to exploding.

I needed to try to concentrate on just one step at a time.

"What did you mean by a labyrinth, exactly?" I asked. *Would the king be bloodthirsty enough to put his own sons into real mortal danger?* If their lives were put at serious risk, ours would be too—assuming they were planning to keep us alongside them throughout the contest, which was a logical assumption based on everything Tejus had said so far.

Tejus allowed himself to display a clear flicker of impatience now. "As I told you," he said pointedly, "we have not been told exactly what it involves."

"But would your father put your lives at real risk?" I pressed.

"I would not put it past him," Tejus replied shortly.

I swallowed hard. *Great.*

I knew enough about supernaturals to know that not all of them made good parents like mine did. Some of them could be harsh, callous, brutal... which often explained the temperament of the offspring they produced.

"So, what I'm getting at here is, myself and my brother and friends—our lives could be put at risk?" I asked.

"Not as much risk as ours—if there is true risk," Tejus replied, "because, in case you haven't guessed, it will be in my and my brothers' best interests to keep you alive as long as possible. You will be a source of strength to us within the labyrinth, and without you we don't stand as great a chance of succeeding... It was our father himself who advised us to seek out humans as cohorts for the trials ahead. He has known of their value to our kind for a long time now. Thus, it was at his recommendation that we headed to the human realm to begin with."

"Known of their value." Again, it prickled me to hear Tejus speak of humans as though we were commodities. These sentries were still living in the dark ages in terms of species equality... and something told me that I would have a hard, long road ahead of me if I ever wanted to turn Tejus—or any of these people—around.

"So," he concluded, scooping up his lynx from the ground and propping it on his shoulder. "Do you accept my proposal?"

"What other choice do I have?"

"None," he admitted. "But I should like to have your formal agreement all the same."

I wasn't sure I wanted to give him that, but I ended

up nodding bitterly. "You'd better release my brother and friends if you win," I said through clenched teeth.

"Certainly," he said, reaching the door. "If *we* win... I have some matters to attend to now, but I will be back for you soon to explain our next step—I suggest you try to rest a little while I'm gone..."

With that, he opened the door and stalked out.

"Wait!" I said, hurrying to the door and wedging my foot through its gap just before he could close it. "I want to see my brother and friends."

"Oh, you will," he said. "Trust me, you will."

"When?" I demanded.

"Soon. I promise." Then he nudged my foot out of the way and closed the door before locking it.

My stomach felt like it couldn't sink any lower as I staggered away from the door and sank down on the chaise-longue.

Fear and uncertainty throbbed in my brain.

I had no idea what we'd just gotten ourselves into, but there was one thing I did know:

This was a game Tejus and I could not afford to lose.

Even if the result of his winning was that I got thrust deeper into this mysterious and frightening world of sentries, for the sake of my brother, Ruby, Julian and—eventually—myself, Tejus had to win.

Getting Tejus through his first test was our only hope of escape.

Chapter 10: Hazel

I was relieved that Tejus kept his promise. What felt like fifteen minutes later—I couldn't be sure exactly how much time had passed because my watch had strangely stopped working—the door to my chamber swung open again, and in stepped a tall (over six foot) wiry woman wearing what was clearly the garb of a servant, a plain brown smock with a wraparound apron, her sleek black hair wrapped in a severe bun. She looked quite elderly, her lips shriveled and lined.

"Prince Tejus has requested his brothers to allow a meeting with your fellow humans as a courtesy to you all," she announced. "And they agreed. So I ask you to come with me. I will lead you to them."

That was somewhat decent of him, at least. It did little to raise my estimation of him though.

I hardly needed to be asked twice. I rushed to the door, in such a hurry I almost tripped over my feet as I staggered out into a long dark hallway. The walls were made of deep gray stone, like in my sitting room, and aside from some carpets and several coats of copper arms and swords adorning the walls like trophies, it was bare.

I could hardly contain my anticipation as she led me down a winding staircase. We arrived in another hallway, lined with old wooden doors—all of them tall enough for sentries to fit through. We stopped outside one of them. She clutched the handle and pushed it open with a low creak, and the next thing I knew I was stepping into a small hall with a concave ceiling and a long oaken table… around which sat three familiar faces.

I practically cried with relief as I ran to them. They

leapt from their chairs instantly. I first drew Benedict into a stifling embrace—his face was so pale with fear, his cheeks so cold—before moving on to hold Ruby and Julian, who had been sitting on either side of my brother.

"Oh, God," Ruby gasped. Her long blonde hair was matted, her expression strained and exhausted. Julian looked no less ruffled.

"How have you been holding up?" I asked them in a hushed tone, as I threw a glance back over my shoulder to make sure that the maid had closed the door. She had, leaving us with what I hoped was some privacy. "They haven't tried to crack into any of your minds yet, have they?" I asked, terrified by the thought.

"What does that even mean?" Benedict asked.

It struck me that their captors might not have been as talkative as Tejus was… or perhaps they hadn't been gutsy enough—or stupid enough, depending on how you looked at it—to provoke answers from the brothers. Julian and Ruby looked just as clueless as Benedict about our situation. Poor things.

I proceeded to explain everything Tejus had revealed to me and by the time I was done, their faces had paled even further and they'd practically stopped breathing.

"Sentries," Julian said hoarsely. "Who would have guessed."

"We couldn't have," Ruby whispered. "Nobody could."

"And there we were being good kids doing what our parents told us," Benedict croaked. "We would have been better off sneaking off to Hawaii."

At least my brother still had some sense of humor left in him. All three had assured me—after I'd explained the difference between sentries "testing" a human's mind and cracking into it—that their minds hadn't been cracked or broken. In fact, Benedict and Julian hadn't even spoken to their sentries. They'd just found themselves waking up in a strange room, like I had. As for Ruby, she'd spoken to hers and experienced that weird feeling of him "feeding" on her mental energy—but he hadn't revealed nearly as much as Tejus had to me.

I let out an unsteady sigh. It seemed that, no matter what Shadians did, they always found some way to get caught up in a mess.

Ugh. Life is so much simpler in a sports romance novel…

My mind drifted back to that story even now, and I felt all the more justified for avoiding all things supernatural in the books I read. I could do with a good dose of normality at present to steady my nerves, but I had something urgent to discuss with the trio. I didn't know how long we'd be allowed to remain in here together. I dreaded the door opening again and us being pulled our separate ways.

I wrapped my arms around them as they sat next to me at the table and pulled our heads in close, so that I could speak as softly as possible… I still feared somebody might be eavesdropping at the door and I wasn't sure how sharp sentries' hearing was—whether it was any sharper than humans'. I assumed that it was, given Tejus's brief comment about humans' inferior eyesight back in the chamber.

"We've got to find a way to make sure that Tejus gets to the sword first," I told them. Any kind of strategy was insanely difficult to plan out because I still didn't know what this trial would involve. "Somehow, you've got to find subtle ways to slow your sentry down, if you suspect that you are gaining speed on Tejus and me. If any of you reaches the sword first—we will have no escape in sight."

Even as I spoke, I became aware of Tejus' cleverness once again. Giving me this incentive of saving my three companions, and arranging this meeting for us, couldn't have been more in line with his own objectives. He'd probably already planned this out before he walked into the room to talk to me—and that was probably why he'd bothered to answer my questions and be somewhat amenable. He wanted me on his side, so I would get Benedict, Ruby and Julian on my side… thus thwarting his brothers and making it more likely he'd reach the sword first.

I doubted his fourth brother would pose a threat to him if he failed to find a suitable human—the chances of which were extremely unlikely. Tejus had already said they'd searched the human realm for some time with no luck in finding "the right minds".

Tejus really is a smart ass. Like those arrogant smart alecks you read about in love stories… though, unlike those characters, I doubted he had a romantic or redeemable underbelly.

"If Tejus wins, you will be left here all alone!" Benedict said in a pained voice.

I gripped his shoulder and looked him firmly in the eye. "That's still better than all four of us being left here. If you get taken back to the human realm and return to our family, there's a chance you can come back for me." *Somehow… someday…* and hopefully I would still be alive by then.

He gulped, his lips trembling slightly.

"You've got to be strong for me, Benedict, and for all of us," I told him, while I tried to maintain my own strength—or at least show of strength. "But at the same time"—my eyes swept to Ruby and Julian—"you've got to stay safe. Your sentries *cannot* figure out that you're working against them. Who knows what they would do if they did… They might even want to kill you."

A pause of tense silence ensued. This was going to be the hardest thing any of us had ever had to do in our lives. None of us—being humans—had ever been directly involved with TSL's (and later GASP's) supernatural struggles. We'd merely watched from the sidelines while tucked safely away in The Shade. Now we'd been thrown into a boiling pot, with no knowledge or preparation, and forced to fight for our lives.

But there was a reason why the sentries had singled us out from the other humans. We were different. We were tough, in spite of our inexperience. We were children of fighters. Of survivors. Surviving against all odds ran in our blood. We would find a way. We had to.

Each of us seemed to come to the same somber

conclusion as we eyed each other, and the three of them nodded at me.

"We'll just have to do the best we can," Ruby said.

"Play it by ear," Julian added.

"And hope we'll be able to gain a sense of where each of us is once we're in the mystery maze," Benedict said worriedly. "If we have no idea of each other's whereabouts… that could really screw things up."

"Well, in that case," I said, "you've just got to do all you can to slow them down anyway, even if Tejus and I are way ahead."

We also had to hope none of the sentries broke into our minds. If they did that, the game would be over.

"Do we even know *when* the trial will start?" Benedict asked.

I didn't, but before I could answer, the sound of the door creaking behind us echoed through the hall. I pursed my lips as we turned and saw the maid standing there. It seemed that our time was up.

"I believe your lords are expecting you back now," she announced, making her way toward us.

Lords, huh. So that's what they fancy themselves as... There were a lot of things I'd like to call Tejus in this moment, but *Lord* wasn't one of them.

She ushered Benedict, Ruby and Julian away from the table, and I was about to follow when the woman turned to me. "Your lord is not ready for you yet. I was addressing the others."

Benedict left the maid's side and flung himself into my arms. I hugged him tight, and then exchanged an emotional hug goodbye with Julian and Ruby, before the three of them were escorted out of the room.

Good luck... I bade them in my mind as the door closed with chilling finality behind them.

In many ways, their task was a lot more risky than mine. I didn't have to hide anything from Tejus. I just had to do what I could to help him reach the sword—whatever that was going to involve. But the others would have to actively look for ways to sabotage their sentries' progress...

We were going to need courage and tenacity if we were ever going to see the other end of this tunnel, without a doubt. But more than that, we were going to need luck.

A lot of luck.

Chapter 11: Hazel

When Tejus entered the hall to collect me a few minutes later, I eyed him with disdain. He'd come without his lynx friend.

"Thought it would be courteous to grant me and my 'fellow humans' a little reunion, did you?" I said in a low tone.

He frowned, feigning ignorance, but I knew the cogs were turning in his brain. He reached my side by the table and looked down at me, crossing his arms. "Would you prefer to not have had a reunion, then?" he asked pleasantly. "Because I certainly could have arranged for that too."

I scowled and looked away from him. There was no point in responding. I'd just made the comment to let him know that I saw through him, and out of irritation. I didn't like the feeling of being played. I was going to be more alert with him now though, conscious of everything he did and said in an attempt to understand his real motives.

"I'd like to take you to my quarters now," he said, holding out an arm to me. Then he nodded toward the door. "Shall we?"

I rejected his arm and began striding toward the door. With his long legs, he swiftly caught up with me and reached the door before I did. He opened it for me and allowed me to step out first.

As we moved down the corridor, I fell back a step. Whether I was walking in front of him or behind him, I didn't much care. I just didn't want to be level with him.

"When will the trial begin?" I asked him.

"I will inform you," he said.

He didn't say another word as we wound back up the staircase the maid had led me down. Only we ventured much higher. Higher and higher until my legs were aching. I'd gained some perspective on the height of this building when I'd looked out of the window, but these stairs almost seemed to be playing tricks on me. Just when I thought it would be impossible for another set of stairs to emerge, they did. I almost regretted not taking Tejus' arm so that I could lean on him and let him carry my weight… but not quite.

Finally, we stopped on a landing. Tejus' breathing hadn't quickened in the slightest. His pulse seemed barely different than it had been when he'd been walking on flat ground. He took a right turn and we passed more shadowy doorways until he stopped outside of one of them. I'd noticed that the carpets on this floor seemed thicker, richer. More luxurious. A sign of the royal quarters, I guessed. The handle of the door he pushed open was also made of what looked like silver, and the wood his door was constructed from looked less worn, more polished.

He stepped into a heavily carpeted corridor whose walls were adorned with the skulls of some kind of very large predatory bird. Maybe from the type of vultures I'd seen flapping around near the base of the castle.

Perhaps they were a sign of dominance in sentry culture. Domineering or not, they looked creepy as hell.

As we neared the end of the long corridor (which I noticed was scattered with lynx hairs) Tejus led me through another doorway, into a spacious, comfortable-looking sitting room. The shutters of the tall windows that lined one of the walls were all open, letting in the final, dying embers of sunlight. The thought that it would be night soon made me shudder. This castle was spooky enough already.

I was expecting Tejus to ask me to take a seat on one of the large, deep red, velvety couches, but instead he continued leading me through the room to the other side.

He reached an old bookcase and, gripping its edges, pulled it aside to reveal a tapestry depicting two vultures battling in the sky. Then he pulled that aside too. My lips parted as I found myself staring at what was apparently a secret doorway. A tiny stone doorway—too low even for me to walk through without ducking.

"What the…"

My voice trailed off as he pushed it open with a low grinding noise. He ducked and moved through it, obviously expecting me to follow. As I arrived on the other side, I found myself in a small round room filled with low tables containing glowing green stones. Yeah, I wasn't hallucinating. They were luminescent emerald crystals.

"What are these?" I whispered as I approached the nearest cluster. I bent down to stare at them. *And why are you hiding them?*

"They're a, uh, collection of mine," Tejus said after grinding the stone door closed—which made me kind of nervous, given how tiny this room was. He approached and bent down with me before picking up one of the crystals and handing it to me.

Its surface was rough and scratchy, yet as it made contact with my skin, I felt an odd spread of warmth trickle through my arm and up my shoulder, toward my chest.

Unnerved, I instantly put it back down on the table. *What kind of magic is this?*

"You didn't answer my question," I reminded him, looking him in the eye. His focus was on the stones, their green light reflecting in his dark irises and making them glimmer.

Tejus rose, and since the ceiling was low—not quite as low as the door but still not nearly high enough for him to stand—he was forced to hunch. "You can call them energy stones," he said after a moment of thought. "Though they weren't always this way. They started out as regular stones I gathered from Luckafew Peak—I collected them for their absorbent properties. Over time, I managed to infuse them with my own energy, and I keep them here for times when I am running low on outside sources of energy and need additional strength. I simply have to make sure that I re-infuse them again for the next time that I need them."

Like rechargeable batteries.

"So why have you brought me in here?" I asked. "Why are you showing these to me? Aren't these, like, your prized possessions? Why would you trust me with their whereabouts?"

"Because you are going to sleep here tonight."

I thought that had to be some kind of joke, but his face was dead serious as he spoke.

"What?"

"I will bring in some bedding and lay it down on the floor for you. You will be perfectly comfortable."

I looked around the dark, pokey room, glowing with the eerie green stones, and curled my nose. "Why would you want me to sleep in here?"

"The stones will grant you additional mental energy overnight," he said, "and that is important, for my father has decided that, since four of his sons have found human cohorts and his fifth is unlikely to find one any time soon, tomorrow shall be the Day of the Labyrinth. We will leave in the morning."

My heart skipped a beat as I stared at him.

"You need to harness as much mental energy as you can," he said, gazing down at me intently. His hair had come loose from his ponytail due to the way he was bending, and it grazed the sides of his face. "You need to become like my energy stone."

I didn't like the idea of becoming anyone's *energy stone*, least of all Tejus'.

"Well… why don't you just, I don't know," I spluttered, "get yourself a sack and sling some of these stones over your shoulder—carry them with you in the labyrinth? Why do you even need me in the first place? Why do you need any of us? Don't your brothers have this too?"

He frowned in disdain.

Okay, the image of Tejus lugging around all these stones around a maze was kind of ludicrous. But I was still curious to hear his answer.

"Even leaving aside the impracticality of it," he replied, "these stones cannot remain potent outside of this small, enclosed environment. Away from the wind, the light, from all interfering outside elements. Even if they could, they wouldn't come close to the energy you could provide me, as a warm, strong-minded human. As for my brothers… I doubt any of them have thought of this."

And you're obviously not going to ever inform them of this tactic.

I was filled with a somewhat sick feeling as I thought about what kind of relationship these brothers must have. They could hardly even be called brothers, given the way they were pitted against each other. I'd seen how Tejus had whipped out a sword against one of them, when he had lunged for me at the same time as Tejus back on Murkbeech Island. And now they would do all they could to beat their brothers in the maze and reach the sword first.

I looked around the room again, this time with

resignation. "Okay," I muttered. "So you want me to sleep in this hole tonight." Somehow I doubted I'd do any sleeping. I had a hard enough time dozing off in strange places as it was—even back in the Murkbeech dorm—not to speak of this weird place.

"I can have Lucifer keep you company, if you like."

A chill stole down my spine. "Lucifer?" I breathed.

What, is this guy some kind of devil-worshipper now? He kind of looked like the type—long hair, bird skulls on his wall, his creepy…

"My feline," Tejus clarified.

"O-Oh." I almost heaved a sigh of relief. "Uh, no. Definitely not."

Having that creepy yellow-eyed cat staring at me all night would hardly help. Least of all now that I'd been informed his name was Lucifer. *Who names a cat Lucifer?* Or maybe the name wasn't associated with the devil in sentry culture. Maybe they didn't even believe in the devil… I sensed there was enough evil lurking in this place as it was.

I wondered if I'd offended Tejus by my abrupt rejection of his cat. If I had, he didn't show it.

He retreated out of the cubby hole, back into the sitting room. I followed him and waited by the stone entrance as he crossed the sitting room and disappeared into the corridor. He returned less than a minute later with a handful of bedding: what looked like a thick woolen blanket, a cushion and a feather mattress. I stepped aside so he could move back into the stone room, where he laid down the bedding for me. Then he stepped out again and looked down at me, before gesturing to the room.

"Your bed is made."

I moved reluctantly inside and approached the bed. I pressed a hand down against the mattress. It was surprisingly soft considering how thin it was.

The door ground behind me, and as I turned again, Tejus was closing the door.

"Wait," I said, suddenly feeling like a kid afraid of the dark. I placed my palms against the surface of the door and said, "Can't you leave this door open? Even a bit ajar?"

Tejus shook his head. "I cannot. The door must be kept closed to preserve the stones."

My throat tightened as he proceeded to push the door until it closed, all light from the outside blocked out, leaving me bathed in green.

Trying not to look around the room, I slipped beneath the blanket and pulled it up over my head before curling up into a fetal position.

I missed my home. My bed. My family.

I missed The Shade.

Chapter 12: Hazel

It was difficult to fall asleep, but once I managed it I slept surprisingly soundly. One good thing about the small room was that it was completely quiet; the creepy light might have disturbed me at first, but at least there were no creepy sounds to accompany it.

As morning drew in, I had fallen into a very deep slumber. I woke up only due to a pinching in my bladder. I got a shock when I first opened my eyes, having completely forgotten where I was, but then I remembered. I'd slept in here to "recharge". As I rose to my feet, I tried to detect whether I felt any different. And I soon realized that I did, once the cobwebs of sleep had lifted from me. My brain felt sharp, clear, quick. Like I'd just taken a bath in ice cold water.

I moved to the door while realizing that I had no idea where the bathroom was in this apartment. Pressing my hands against the heavy stone, I pushed hard, praying that Tejus hadn't locked it. He hadn't. It was a lot of effort, but gradually it ground open, allowing me to slide out into the sun-streaked sitting room. After closing the door again—remembering what Tejus had told me about the stones needing enclosure—I moved to one of the tall windows and gazed out over the land that surrounded us, my eyes passing over the sun itself. The same mist hung over the city as last night, and to my surprise, the sun actually wasn't all that much brighter. It still had a hazy, subdued quality, and was more peachy-orange in color than brilliant yellow like the sun I was used to on Earth.

I moved away from the window and as I crossed the living room, I spotted a steel platter with a domed lid perched on a low table by the seating in the center of the room. Next to it was a jug and a goblet. Approaching it, I raised the platter's lid—clearly breakfast left for me. A portion of thick, glutinous stew and some kind of grainy, dark brown bread. I was starving, so as dubious as the food looked, I found myself kneeling in front of the table, filling the goblet with water from the jug and taking a bite of the meal. The food was as disgusting as it looked—thick, bland, hard to swallow. It tasted a bit like barley—both the stew and the bread, and worst of all salt seemed to be an ingredient that was completely absent. After finishing the platter, it sat heavily in my stomach. I couldn't complain that it wasn't filling.

Then I left the living room in search of a bathroom. Entering the corridor that led directly to the front door, I poked my head through all the doorways I passed—not spotting Tejus anywhere, though his lynx was prowling near the front door—until I came across what I was looking for. Toilet facilities. I shut myself inside the room—disconcerted that there was no lock—and relieved myself quickly, before moving to a metal water basin to splash water on my face and rinse my mouth in an attempt to freshen myself. There was a weird porcelain tub of green goo beside the basin. It smelt strong and spicy; I guessed it was derived from some kind of plant. Toothpaste for sentries, apparently. I dipped a finger in it and brushed my teeth as best as I could. The substance caused a tingling and a burning sensation as it made contact with my gums. At least I felt fresh afterward.

I left the bathroom and stood in the corridor. "Tejus?" I called.

I wondered what time it was. We were supposed to be leaving for the labyrinth—wherever that was—in the morning, weren't we? I took that as meaning early in the morning.

I continued looking around his quarters—poking

my head through doors that were ajar while attempting to push open those that weren't—all the while calling out his name. But I couldn't find him anywhere.

Strange.

I dared to move to the front door and attempt to open it. No chance. It was locked.

As I backed away, I almost tripped over Lucifer, who bared his fangs and hissed at me again.

I rolled my eyes at him before returning to the sitting room. I guessed Tejus would return soon enough. Maybe he was downstairs with his brothers having breakfast, or having some kind of final word with his father. Maybe even a briefing.

I ended up sitting on the couch and watching the lynx as I waited. He moved over to me, still looking at me distrustfully, and decided to settle on the couch opposite me. The two of us sat in stiff silence until, finally, the main door pushed open.

Lucifer and I leapt from the couch and hurried down the corridor to find Tejus emerging. He was wearing a kind of suit—it consisted of a long-sleeved black top with a stiff collar and straight black pants. And in one pocket of his shirt was a deep red rose. As he moved in, he discarded the rose on a ledge near the doorway before glancing toward me and his lynx.

"What's happening?" I asked him, frowning.

His long hair was tied back again, matching his smart appearance. His expression was strangely ashen as he replied, "There was a delay this morning. An unexpected funeral."

"What? Funeral?"

"My brother, Danto. He… took his life overnight. He was spotted in the early hours of this morning, hanging from a spire in the courtyard beneath his bedroom window."

I stopped breathing. "Which human was 'his'?" I asked.

"The blonde girl," he replied, peeling off his black jacket to reveal a white shirt beneath.

Ruby. "Is she okay?" I asked.

"Yes," he replied, sweeping past me and toward his

bedroom. "She will now be given to Jenus… the brother of mine who failed to find a human of his own, and who returned to Nevertide last night."

The one who had leapt for me.

"Are you sure it was suicide?" I asked tentatively, not wanting to outright accuse one of his brothers of murder. But come on. The humanless brother returned the night before the labyrinth trial, and by the morning one of his human-equipped brothers was dead?

As Tejus entered his bedroom and pushed the door ajar, I waited outside. I figured he might be changing or something. There was a long pause before he emerged again, wearing a shabbier pair of pants. He had also strapped a thick belt to his waist, attached to which were a line of five sheathed daggers and two long swords.

"My father has accepted it as a suicide," he said, his voice steady and unfeeling. "And that is all that matters."

I stared after him as he headed toward the front

door. What was that supposed to mean? Perhaps the king favored Jenus over Danto. That was the only logical way to explain this situation. There was no way Danto would commit suicide the night before what must have been one of the most important tests of his life. He had a human. He had probably been raring to start the quest for his chance to compete for the crown.

I wondered how the king would explain it to others who weren't his sons or directly related to him—like his courtiers, or heck, the public in general. Surely the death of a prince was a major event throughout the kingdom.

Maybe he would weave a story of Danto being unstable, that he had cracked under the pressure and all that was at stake during the next day's events.

I shuddered to think what kind of monster Tejus' father must be.

And what did Tejus think of all this? What was going through his mind? Although he was somber, he didn't appear to be shocked by what happened.

It made me wonder what had happened to his mother, as well as whether he used to have more brothers than I was aware of.

At least Ruby was safe.

I clenched my fists as Tejus beckoned me out of the front door with him and into the hallway outside.

Fear gripped me imagining Ruby now being forced to submit to Jenus.

But more than anything now, I feared for all of our lives.

If Jenus had killed once to get his way—and killed his own brother at that—what would stop him from killing again?

Chapter 13: Hazel

Tejus led me down hundreds of steps until we reached far lower than I'd ever gone in the castle—a torchlit basement whose walls were bedecked with shelf upon shelf of weapons. There were swords, spears, bludgeons, clubs… Tejus snatched up a spear before moving over to a bow-and-arrow stand.

"Uh, what do you think you will need all this for?" I murmured.

"There could be anything within the labyrinth," he replied, not turning around. "And I mean anything… Or it could turn out that I don't need weapons at all and I will have wasted my time in gathering them. I must be prepared for all circumstances."

"Will you meet your brothers before we leave?" I asked, though of course what I really wanted to know was whether I would have a moment with my brother, Ruby and Julian again before we departed.

Before Tejus could reply, footsteps sounded outside. They echoed closer until the door to the armory swung open, and in stepped Tejus' three brothers. The last time I'd seen them had been in the darkness of Murkbeech Island. Though I instantly recognized Jenus. All the brothers looked fairly similar—the same russet-brown hair and dark, almost black eyes—but Jenus' features struck me as harder, harsher, colder than the others'—even more than Tejus', now that I saw him in clear light.

Ruby, Julian and Benedict had entered with them and I was relieved to see them again, even if none of us would find the opportunity to talk.

Tejus didn't appear to intend to talk much—or at

all—to his brothers. He barely even turned to acknowledge their entrance in the room as they began milling about the shelves, equipping themselves with arms. I could only guess that we were due to leave very soon.

As my eyes fell on Jenus again, I could hardly blame Tejus for wanting to play as dirty as he could and use his cunning to his full advantage. Jenus clearly had no qualms about anything, and though I could not speak for the others, I suspected that they hadn't fallen too far from the tree.

You wouldn't know from any of their expressions that their brother had been discovered gruesomely killed just a few hours ago. None of them were smiling, but they seemed to have returned to business as usual.

I swallowed hard as I returned my focus to what Tejus was doing. He had apparently finished arming himself—he'd started to move faster as soon as his brothers entered the room. He clearly didn't feel comfortable in their presence.

He caught my eye briefly and nodded toward the door, but we'd barely taken five steps across the armory when his brother Jenus spoke up. "Father wants us to wait down here for him." His voice was nasally and scratchy—unpleasant in a way that Tejus' wasn't.

Tejus' Adam's apple bobbed as he stalled. He let out a slight breath before moving backward and leaning against a patch of wall that wasn't totally covered by weapons—something that was quite a rarity in this room.

The king. I felt nervous at the prospect of seeing him. I joined Tejus in leaning against the wall, while my eyes roamed my brother, Ruby and Julian. I was particularly concerned as I examined Ruby's expression, trying to understand her state of mind. Jenus had better not do anything nasty to her, or if we ever did manage to get The Shade's army here, I would personally ensure that he was the first to pay.

Ruby definitely looked more terrified than the last time I'd seen her, but that was only to be expected.

She had the vision of a dead body still fresh in her mind. That wasn't something that could be erased easily.

More footsteps sounded—more than one person was approaching. The door opened again, and this time in the doorway stood a man as tall as Tejus… but their height was about the only similarity I could spot between the two. Atop his bald head was a golden crown and he wore a long sweeping cloak. His eyes were a sharp blue color, rather than black-brown, and around his jaw and mouth was a heavy beard which more than made up for the lack of hair on his head—it trailed down to graze the top of his chest. His expression was serious as he looked about the room, though there was a slight gleam in his eye that shouldn't have been there as his focus rested on Jenus. Perhaps Jenus was the favorite son. Perhaps the king had even been a part of the conspiracy to end Danto. Maybe Danto had done something to anger him. Who knew what was going through his head.

He barely paid any attention to us humans, other than a brief glance—which I couldn't exactly complain about.

"Are you prepared to depart?" he asked, his tone rich and throaty.

The brothers nodded.

"Then let us leave," he said. "Your obstacles within the labyrinth have already been set in motion in anticipation of today. As much as we mourn the loss of Danto, I'm sure that even he would want us to proceed… We have a kingdom to retain for our lineage and time is drawing to a close."

I felt sick to my stomach looking at the man. One would have thought that the death of a son should be enough to take at least a week off for mourning. Not in Hellswan Kingdom—where apparently politics and cunning ruled over emotion or, heck, just common decency.

The king swept out of the room. Tejus allowed his brothers to leave next with Ruby, Julian and my brother and then we followed. I realized only now that the king had been accompanied by two stockily built cronies. We wound our way back up the castle, and this time, I did reach out to grab Tejus' arm. If he was going to drag me on this mission, he might as well drag me up the stairs too.

I let him carry most of my weight as I clung on to him and leaned against him, until we finally left the staircase. We passed along a hallway and took a right turn through a door. We crossed a cavernous hall filled with chairs—some kind of meeting room, or auditorium. And when we reached the end of this, a doorway into the outside world came into view. Hazy sunlight spilled through it, beckoning us out.

The king and his two men still at the lead, they descended a wide flight of steps that led down to a familiar courtyard. It was scattered with small clusters of leafless trees, and in one corner was the cage of vultures I'd spotted from the window of the room I first woke up in.

As we gathered around the cage, it was clear what our mode of transport would be.

The king withdrew a key from his pocket and thrust it into the door of the cage. He twisted and a sharp click followed. Then the door swung open. Ruby, Julian, my brother and I gasped and leapt back at once as the vultures immediately flew forward in an attempt to escape.

The brothers moved inside and a few seconds later, the vultures had become tame, docile, malleable. More of their mind control at work.

Each of the brothers grabbed hold of collars that were tied around the birds' necks and pulled them out of the cage. Then the two cronies stepped inside and collected three more—one of which they passed to the king.

I exchanged nervous glances with Benedict, Julian and Ruby. It looked like we were going to be riding these birds freestyle.

The sentries mounted the vultures, swinging their long legs over each bird's side, before the brothers each held a hand down to pull us up. I gripped hold of Tejus' forearm tensely as he jerked me upward. I sat behind him on the vulture's feathery back and found myself forced to cling on to him for dear life as the bird's wings spread and jerked us upward with barely a second's warning. My arms snaked around Tejus' muscled waist, the front of me pressing flush against his back. My heart was racing as we rose higher and higher. There was nothing stopping me from falling—the strength of my grip around Tejus was my only safety. As I caught sight of Benedict and his sentry flying shortly behind us, my fear consumed me. *Hold on, little brother. Hold on.*

It didn't help that the flight was so bumpy. These vultures really weren't the most graceful of birds. They darted up and down, varying their altitude erratically, almost as though they were deliberately testing how firmly we were holding on. Perhaps Tejus sensed my fear, for he turned his head slightly as his hands dug into the feathers behind the bird's neck.

"You can sit in front of me if you'd feel safer," he offered.

I declined. I was too scared to attempt to change

positions now that we were mid-flight… and besides, it would feel weird being so engulfed by Tejus, his arms and legs enveloping me.

Thus I remained clinging to the sentry. Even with such weight on their backs, the birds were able to fly far faster than any bird I'd ever witnessed in the human realm. Almost dragon speed.

I wasn't able to concentrate on the ground below—how much progress we had made since leaving the palace, or whether I could spot any sign of the labyrinth in the distance. It was all I could do to simply hold on. Making myself acutely aware of the height at which we were flying would only make the experience ten times more terrifying.

I only got a clue that we were nearing our destination when the king barked a command to his sons. "Start flying low! We don't want any of you getting a special advantage as to the labyrinth's contents…"

Yeah, right.

Tejus made us descend, and so did the others…

though Jenus was the last to obey his father, clearly hoping to gain some small advantage.

I felt the bird soaring lower and lower, and then I finally mustered the courage to look beneath us.

We had completely passed over the vast stretch of kingdom I had beheld yesterday from the window. The buildings, the roads, the patches of agricultural land… now we were nearing what appeared to be a rocky wasteland—except for a wide patch of green looming in the distance.

The labyrinth.

Perhaps it was just my nerves, but we suddenly seemed to be closing the distance much faster. The next thing I knew, I could make out details of the maze. It was a massive area—so vast that I couldn't even see the end of it—though if we had still been flying high the end may have been visible. I wondered how they had even created such a place in the first place. The maze was so at odds with its surroundings—its walls dense with giant thorns and tightly wound vegetation grown so high that five sentries standing on top of each other wouldn't have been able to see over the top. The rest of the terrain was dry, dusty, painted with hues of brown, almost like a desert. It was like the labyrinth had sprung up here by way of magic. It made me wonder whether the king might have an alliance with a magic-wielder after all—a rogue jinni or a witch, perhaps.

Whatever the case, I wasn't left with much time to mull it over. The vultures took a sudden dive, and then we had all landed on the parched ground with a thump that almost caused me to go flying off the vulture. I slipped off its sleek feathery back, my knees feeling weak as my feet touched solid ground. My eyes immediately shot toward my brother and two friends. They had landed safely too, thank God.

Turning to face the thorny exterior wall of the maze, I realized that there were five wooden doorways into it, spread about eight feet apart.

"You will each enter through one of them," the king announced. "They will take you on parallel but separate paths through the labyrinth. The sword lies deep within the maze. I will post my men in the sky to hover and monitor you, to ensure no foul play goes on," he added.

Yeah, right, I thought again.

Though this could make it more difficult for my brother, Julian and Ruby to attempt to slow their sentries down. However they tried to do it, they'd have to be careful that the watchers wouldn't detect any foul play from *them*.

The king's eyes passed over his sons. "I know that, whatever the outcome of this trial, each of you will do me—and your kingdom—proud… May the best man win."

Then he gestured toward the doors, indicating that we head to them.

Is that all their father is going to tell them before thrusting them into this?

Perhaps some other meeting had taken place before now that I didn't know about, because none of the sentries looked surprised.

As we all took positions outside the entrances, my

palms were sweating. I eyed my brother and friends anxiously one last time before the sentries opened the doors and we stepped inside.

We emerged at the beginning of a long, shadowed path, just wide enough for two people to walk side by side. Tejus's hand moved immediately to his spear, which he had fastened to his belt with a clip. He held it out in front of him, as the wooden door swung shut behind us. I could hear the others on either side of us—their feet crunching over the ground—beginning to roam down the path. Tejus didn't lose time either. Meeting my gaze, he looked at me sharply before nodding to move ahead.

"What are the rules?" I asked. "There must be some? And will our paths cross at all with the others? Will we be constantly traveling parallel to them?"

"We are not supposed to cross paths for a while," Tejus said. "At least according to what my father shared with us earlier this morning, after the funeral. He said we may cross paths at some point though, as we get deeper into the maze. As for rules, my father discussed that with us earlier too. None of us are to harm each other, or our humans. That would not be fair play. Our father has stated that the obstacles are designed to test our tenacity and durability—both things we will need in surplus if we are to stand a chance of taking the crown."

I wasn't sure I really believed that. I guessed only time would tell, as we wound deeper into the maze and stress levels got higher. At least Tejus was well armed, and, as he'd indicated, he was supposed to be a fine swordsman. It unnerved me that I didn't have any weapon at all on my person though. For all I knew a monster could come bursting from the shadows and hurtling toward us at any moment.

"Can I have one of your weapons?" I asked him.

"There's no point. I need to start carrying you now anyway or we will be putting ourselves at a disadvantage."

He lowered himself to his knees, quickly beckoning me to climb onto his back. Clutching his shoulders, I did so carefully. As he rose, I tucked my legs around him to make sure I wasn't going to slip off. Then he began to run.

"H-How long is this going to take?"

"I don't know," came his predictable answer. "The faster we go, the sooner we'll be done."

"Has this maze always been here?" I asked, gazing around the thick thorny walls in wonderment.

"No."

"Since how long then?"

"I don't know."

"Well, who put it up here in the first place?"

"Again, I don't know. I have not roamed this side of the kingdom of late."

I huffed in frustration. If it was installed by a witch or other magic-wielder, I would have liked to know in advance.

We fell into silence as we turned a corner, finding ourselves at the beginning of yet another long passage.

Something told me that I was going to be sick of hedges by the end of this.

Chapter 14: Hazel

While Tejus carried me I kept looking up at the sky for the watchers. They didn't seem to be following us the whole time, but rather checking on us sporadically. As for the king, perhaps he had returned to his castle to wait for the result.

As Tejus ran with me, there were a number of directions we could have chosen to go in, but at every turn, Tejus was trying to keep us moving ahead. But where we had to choose between right and left, he just seemed to take a random guess. I was becoming increasingly worried as to how we'd even find our way back out again—but then I supposed that was what the watchers were for. They should spot the winner—hopefully Tejus—retrieve the sword, and then swoop down to help us all get out of here.

Winding deeper and deeper into the eerily quiet maze, I felt more and more nervous. I was on edge the whole time, expecting something to leap out at us at any moment. It became so agonizing, I almost wished something would leap out at us just to break the suspense.

I could no longer hear the footsteps of the others. I guessed that by now we must have distanced ourselves too much. As I found myself wondering if any of them had met with an obstacle yet, a shrill scream pierced the air from somewhere in the distance. It sounded like Ruby's scream.

My heart hammering against my chest, I tightened my grip around Tejus' neck.

Oh, God. What's happened?

Does this mean she and Jenus have already managed

to gain a headstart over us? I hoped that Jenus hadn't caught her trying to slow him down.

We continued venturing forward and I sensed Tejus going more slowly than previously, as if he, too, were fearing what was around the corner. We passed several more twists and turns before arriving at the edge of a clearing. It was a large square patch of grass, which offered three paths to choose from—right, left or straight ahead. Straight ahead was the obvious choice but as Tejus took a step forward into the clearing, the ground suddenly gave way beneath us. We found ourselves falling down, down, down into a shockingly deep earthen pit and landed in a pool of murky water.

During the shock of the fall, Tejus' grip had loosened on me, as my grip had loosened on him. I landed a couple of feet away from him, on my hands and knees in the water—the ground beneath us surprisingly soft—while he had been deft enough to land on his feet.

He reached down to grip my arm and helped me

up. Then we both gazed upward at the distance we'd fallen.

"Well," Tejus said, resuming his stony demeanor. "It looks like we have met with the first task."

He was eyeing the wall closest to us. Leaving my side, he moved toward it. Just as he reached within three feet, razor-sharp blades pierced through the soil so densely that it was impossible to go near the walls now without risking getting spiked.

I wasn't sure what Tejus had been intending to do exactly, perhaps push his hands into the soil and see if he could gain a grip on it to begin climbing upward. Whatever the case, that option was long gone.

"What is going on?" I whispered.

"Goblins," Tejus said.

My heart stopped.

Goblins.

My eyes shot toward where Tejus was gazing—up at the mouth of the hole. Twelve horned greenish creatures about the size of eleven-year-old children had gathered around the hole's entrance and were gazing down at us, their small eyes black as night. Their noses were thin and pointed, their lips wide and thin, revealing the tips of their sharp teeth as they gazed down at us.

I instinctively huddled closer to Tejus as I attempted in vain to even out my breathing.

Then the goblins backed away. This was actually more frightening than if they had continued glaring down at us.

What are they doing now? What the heck is going on?

They did not leave us waiting long. They returned with what appeared to be a circular wooden board, whose diameter looked wide enough to slot perfectly over the entrance of the hole.

A lid.

Attached to its corners were handles, which they were gripping as they cooperated to move it over the hole.

They're going to lock us down here? For what purpose? To see how long we can survive?

Oh, God.

I was fully convinced that they were about to secure the lid over the hole, but as they aligned it perfectly, I realized that it was slightly too small—small enough to fit inside the hole, not quite large enough to cover it. Which meant that if they dropped it, it would come crashing down on top of us.

I was left to wonder what exactly was going through their heads as they flipped it over to reveal the other side of the wood… only no wood was visible. It was covered completely with clusters of tightly-bound vines that were bright red in color. Their leaves resembled ivy a little.

Tejus tensed next to me. "Blood vines," he murmured.

"What?" I choked. "What are blood vines?"

"The most poisonous plant in all of Nevertide—and likely one of the most poisonous in all of the supernatural realm. A single touch against the skin of either human or sentry causes almost instant death."

My mouth pried open as I noticed that one of the goblins had fetched thick rope—which they were quickly winding through the handles… and then the vines were descending: one foot deeper, two feet, three feet.

They stopped abruptly.

I looked to Tejus. His eyes had hardened and glazed over, his lips tightly pursed, his fists clenched. He must have been attempting to control the goblins. Break into their minds. The blood was rising in his otherwise palish face, a vein in his temple pulsing.

I didn't dare speak, and I hardly even breathed, in case I broke Tejus' concentration. I just remained biting my lip so hard it almost bled and praying the vines would start lifting.

After what was probably only five minutes but what felt like half an hour, the vines began to recede. Slowly but surely they raised upward, until the goblins' hands were close to reaching the handles again.

But they never got the chance.

A harrowing snap sounded and the next thing I knew, the vine-infested wooden board was tumbling down toward us at the speed of gravity. My knee-jerk reaction was to instantly drop to the ground, get my head down, even dipping myself underwater, as if that would help me survive the impact in any way.

My life flashed before my eyes. I saw Ruby, Julian and my brother. I saw my parents. All of my family and friends.

A loud splashing noise erupted next to me.

I did not feel any vines or heavy weight upon me. I was not squashed flat. I was still alive.

When I raised myself from the water enough, my eyes fell on Tejus. He had gotten himself into the most bizarre position. He was doing a handstand—his hands deeply embedded in the base of the pool as his heavily booted feet were pressing against the vine-covered circle. I feared that some of the vines could brush against his ankles, but his boots were high.

I was left to gape in awe as Tejus, with the strength

of his arms, began to push the circle backward and then maneuver it into an upright position with his feet… until it was leaning against the blades sticking out from the rounded wall opposite us.

Only once he seemed completely certain that he had secured the circle in place did he dare remove his feet and relinquish his handstand. All the blood had rushed to his head as he stood up and gazed at the circle cautiously.

Then he looked upward.

Apparently during the fall of the circle, he had released his influence on the goblins, because now they were all gathered again around the edges of the circle, ogling us as they had done before.

Then the blades pulled into the walls, leaving holes in the soil. Their suddenly giving way caused the circle to fall back further, but thankfully it looked in no danger of falling upon us.

It seemed that we had completed the obstacle, and were allowed to begin attempting to get out of this hole by other means. But when Tejus once again approached the earthen walls, he didn't have to go so far as to try to gain a grip on the soil. A rope dropped from the heavens. The goblins had chucked it down. Tejus tugged on it firmly, checking the strength of their grip. Then, apparently satisfied, he turned to me and lowered himself, indicating that I resume my position on his back.

My legs were still quivering as I waded my way over. I wrapped my arms around his neck, my legs around his midriff, and clung to him like a monkey as he gripped the rope firmly and climbed up.

I couldn't help but bury my head against the back of his neck as we reached above twenty feet. I didn't want to look down. My limbs were feeling unsteady holding on to him, and watching the distance increase would do nothing to help.

Reaching the entrance, Tejus transferred himself from the rope to the ground and hauled us both out.

The goblins clothed in dark robes parted around him and me, their heads panning upward comically just to be able to look Tejus in the eye. He was incredibly tall by anyone's standards, but a giant compared to these little beasts.

One of them shuffled to the front of the group and placed his gnarled hands on his hips.

"Remember, Tejus Hellswan, that an emperor can never rely solely on his mind for control. He must know how to react fast and instinctively to all types of situations, and be ready to exert all aspects of strength."

As the goblin retreated, Tejus nodded darkly.

I wondered if the creatures had been intentionally supplied with weak rope. Given the goblin's message, it must have all been planned.

Tejus turned his focus to the path that we had intended to take on first entering the clearing—straight ahead, and deeper into the maze.

As he pushed through the crowd of goblins and made his way with me toward it, my nerves were still jittery and frayed.

It was clear as day now that this little *quest* was going to be just as much a test of human tenacity as sentry.

Chapter 15: Hazel

A watcher soared overhead as Tejus carried us onward, before sweeping out of view. My mind was on Jenus. *Where are he and Ruby now?*

Soon we heard the shouting of boys behind us. Julian and my brother, meeting with the same trap at about the same time.

The thought that my brother's life was at the mercy of some complete stranger's reflexes tore me apart, and in that moment, I could no longer think straight.

"The roof will—" I began to bellow out, but before I could finish, Tejus used his supernatural speed to silence me. He twisted me from his back and gripped me hard, holding one hand over my mouth to stifle my shout.

Once I stopped struggling against him, he slowly removed his palm.

"What do you think you're doing?" he hissed, allowing anger to contort his features. "You almost got you and me disqualified!"

I supposed it was just taken for granted that one of the rules was we couldn't communicate with or warn each other about anything.

"If you want to save your human friends, you need to pull yourself together," he said, his intense eyes boring into me. "Lest you want me to begin controlling you."

I gulped hard as he stepped back. Then he turned again and beckoned for me to remount him.

I knew that yelling would have likely made things worse. Based on their shouts, they had already fallen into the pits. The damage had been done. The vines were going to fall. And yelling out would just erase all chances of any of us getting out of here. I hoped that at least they had managed to hear the few words I had managed to call out before Tejus stifled me, and that my unfinished call wouldn't get Tejus and me disqualified.

After what felt like another fifteen minutes had passed, Tejus stopped abruptly again. A chill wind swept up from nowhere and surrounded us, causing the hairs on my body to prickle. And then everything went still.

"What's going on?" I asked him, gazing around.

"I sensed a presence," he said.

"What kind of presence?" I whispered.

"The treacherous kind," was all he replied.

I gulped. *What does that mean?* Tejus passed along several more pathways before he halted once again. His head tilted downward and as I followed his gaze, I almost screamed.

Spread out before us on the ground was the body

of a sentry—a tall female whose dark hair streaked with gray was splayed out all around her. Her body, garbed in a long black dress, ran the width of the passage, her hands—raised above her head—touching the hedge to our right, while her feet touched the hedge to our left.

"What is this?" I breathed.

Tejus had all but stopped breathing too as he gazed down at the corpse. He stepped over it, allowing us both to take in the woman's face. Her eyes were closed, her skin and forehead wrinkly and dry.

"Who is this?" I demanded.

Tejus still didn't respond. He appeared to be in a state of shock, his eyes wide, his lips parted, his breathing becoming hoarse and erratic. This was the greatest amount of emotion I'd seen him let loose since we met.

"My mother," he whispered as he leaned down to touch her shoulder… and as he did, his hand passed right through it. Then the body vanished.

What?

What is this?

My mind felt close to bursting.

Tejus's jaw tightened. He rose to his feet again swiftly, his demeanor changing from shock, and perhaps also sadness, to alertness.

"This is a dervin's work," he said.

"What is a dervin?"

"A devious spirit creature—they are one of the few supernaturals whose minds are very difficult for us to control due to their subtle nature. They are mischief-makers… path-blockers." He surged forward. "We must make haste and attempt to place as much distance between ourselves and it—or them—as possible. Their mental powers are strong—you witnessed the same illusion that I did. Even sentries are not immune to their apparitions."

My arms tightened around Tejus in nervousness. "How do you win over a dervin?"

As we came across another body strewn across the ground—a hallucination of Danto's dead body—it became chillingly clear that we would soon find out. Tejus set me on my feet before looking me seriously in the eye. "I'm going to infuse some of your energy."

I barely had time to brace myself before an extremely uncomfortable sensation rolled through me. It felt almost as though I was being irradiated by him; my brain felt light, my head bloated, my insides wobbly like jelly.

This went on for what felt like an entire minute before he finally stopped.

"Feeling stronger now?" I muttered bitterly. It was a good thing I'd spent the night with those weird energy stones. I had no idea how much energy he was going to have to drain from me throughout this crazy journey. I wondered if it was possible for a human to be drained completely, and what would happen to them.

"Hm," he murmured.

So much for thanks. His sense of entitlement got on my nerves even in this dire situation when I knew he needed to be as strong as possible.

"I don't understand how any of this is a test of *you and your brothers'* capabilities," I told him beneath my breath, "when you're so dependent on us humans… We should be just as much entitled to your rewards."

"We feed, just like any supernatural or human feeds," Tejus replied curtly. I could tell that I had irked him.

I wasn't sure how to counter that though—where to even begin. So I decided not to. We needed to keep an eye out for dervins.

"What do dervins look like?" I asked Tejus.

"They do not usually make themselves seen—only the visions they wish to impart."

I wondered how they were able to "impart" such personal visions. Either the creature had managed to crack Tejus' mind, which I highly doubted, or it had been briefed by the king. It must have been the latter. How the king got a hold of all these other supernatural races was still a mystery to me…

As we reached the end of the current path that we

were traveling along and moved to sweep through an opening in the hedge, an eerie calling drifted down from above us. It sounded like the cackling of a man, or a very deep-throated woman.

"Next will be your bodies lying on the ground, intruders," the voice hissed. "Watch out for them."

I gazed wide-eyed and terrified up at the sky. *What the hell?* Was this creature just trying to mess with our minds, or was it actually intending to kill us?

Tejus withdrew two swords from his belt and held them out in front of him—which confused me. He'd just said that these were subtle creatures.

It was only when I looked toward the opening we were about to pass through that I realized why he'd reached for his weapons. Where there was previously an opening was now thick, thorny hedge. Tejus reached out his blades and brought them down against the hedge that had previously been open space. Although they passed through it, the illusion of hedge remained.

In the next pathway, Tejus dashed for the

turning… only to hit against solid hedge. This thing was messing with us.

"Are you even trying to control it?" I asked him. He'd just drained my mind, so he might as well put my energy to good use.

"Yes," Tejus spat, once again not bothering to control his irritation.

I could see us being at each other's throats by the end of this mission, assuming we both survived it. But as long as he fulfilled his promise, I didn't care. Right now, all I could think about was my friends and brother getting out of here.

It became more and more apparent that the dervin was deliberately attempting to make us lose our sense of direction and go astray. Still, even with my dose of energy running through Tejus, he seemed to be having little luck in controlling it. We kept hitting up against false entryways—and I suspected missing entryways that we should have taken.

I wondered how the others were coping. I still had a creeping fear that Jenus was ahead of us with

Ruby… unless she'd somehow figured out how to slow him down. I hadn't heard her scream in a while.

I had to hope that was a positive thing.

"Keep moving along." The mysterious voice cackled above our heads again, almost giving me a heart attack.

It sounded so close above me, like maybe two feet over my head. I wished in this moment that Tejus wasn't so damn tall.

I felt a chill surround us again.

"You're nearing." The voice came.

Nearing what? I wanted to yell out, but I'd learned my lesson of blurting things out already.

Tejus replaced his swords in his belt and drew out a bow and arrow, apparently thinking it would come in greater use.

"That's right, keep going," spoke the voice. "Keep going, and you shall find it… "

Chapter 16: Ruby

I sensed that Jenus—or Judas, as I called him in my head—had managed to get ahead of Hazel and Tejus when I heard Hazel's scream. After managing to escape the terrifying pit, I knew that I had to do something to slow him down drastically. There was a resolve in his eyes that made me suspect that the pit hadn't been a surprise to him. When we'd fallen, he'd seemed to know exactly what to do. He'd thrust two spears into the base of the pit and held them there firmly as the roof fell… The spears had prevented the roof from reaching us and he'd used them to maneuver the wood into a corner where the red vines could not reach us.

I became convinced that, somehow, he had found out about that first obstacle. Which made me fear what else he might have found out about, what other unfair advantage he might have over his brothers. He might have failed to grab one of us humans from Murkbeech, but he sure didn't have the mindset for failure. He was terrifyingly focused as we passed through the labyrinth.

The problem was, the sentry was insisting on carrying me on his back, so it wasn't like I could feign a twisted ankle. As we darted away from the goblins and moved deeper into the maze, I became so desperate that I let go of his neck and flopped backward. His grip around my legs loosened at the unexpected motion and I went falling painfully to the ground. I managed to stop my head from getting bashed, but given Jenus' height, I did get some significant scrapes and bruises from the rough ground.

"What the hell are you doing?" he asked harshly as

he whipped around and glared down at me. "Useless girl! Get up!"

I pursed my lips and closed my eyes, curling up into a fetal position.

He lowered to scoop me up as I fought against him. "I can't hold on any longer," I breathed, feigning exhaustion. "I'm malnourished and underslept."

He gripped my hair roughly as he jerked my head upright. I winced in pain as he tugged hard against my scalp, forcing me to look him in the eye.

The next thing I knew, his other hand came crashing against the side of my face in a powerful slap that knocked the breath out of me. My cheek stung, my eyes watering as I gazed up at him in anger.

"Did that wake you up?" he spat. He tugged on my hair again, pulling me upright. "Get on my back."

Although I wanted nothing more than to pull one of the daggers from his belt and stab him in the throat, I had no choice but to obey. I had to play this game cautiously. All of our lives were at stake.

I pulled myself back onto him, banging my knees against his hips with more force than was required as I resumed my grip on him, but he didn't seem to notice.

Then he began hurtling forward again. I'd managed to get him to stop for a few seconds. That was hardly going to make a huge impact for Hazel and Tejus.

My pulse quickened as I racked my brain for what else I could possibly do next... then another idea came to me. I waited about ten minutes as we continued rushing through the elaborate maze before saying in a strained voice, "I need to relieve myself... You need to stop again."

"Go on my back if you have to," he growled. "I'm not stopping again."

This man is repulsive.

I bit down hard on my lip. *What else?* I had run out of ideas. The only thing I could think to do was to incur his wrath again by loosening my hold. But I feared I might not be able to do that again without him totally losing it with me.

"How much longer do you think until—?"

I was about to ask how much longer until we came across the next obstacle, when a strange voice spoke above us, accompanied by an uncharacteristically chilly breeze.

"Welcome, welcome…"

"Dervins," Jenus muttered to himself.

"What?" I hissed.

"Keep your mouth shut," he snapped. "I'll tell you if I want you to speak."

I felt like strangling him. *Oh, what my father would do to you if he ever got the chance… or my mother, for that matter.*

I felt a familiar uncomfortable feeling roll through my body as he sapped another dose of my mental energy. I couldn't imagine a more horrible position to find myself trapped in. Not only did I have to put up with the company of this vile man, but he was constantly feeding off me, sucking my energy like a vampire.

As Jenus continued moving forward, bizarrely he started bumping into what appeared to be an open entrance in the hedge. Whatever the heck dervins were, some kind of mysticism was at work here. After taking dozens of missteps, we were eventually led to… a forested area. I hadn't expected to find anything quite like this within the maze. It wasn't small, either, though the trees were as high as the hedges, so I couldn't make out the end of it from where we stood, even atop Jenus' back.

He slipped me to the ground unexpectedly, my feet hitting soil. Then, gripping my shoulder, he thrust me toward the forest.

"You enter first," he commanded.

Wow. Way to respect a lady.

I looked uncertainly at the tightly knit cluster of trees. It was dark inside, and from where I stood, I could barely see past ten feet.

"Uh, what might I find in there?"

"Just do as I say, and enter."

I should have predicted that response.

Drawing in a shuddering breath, I ventured to the entrance of the trees and cautiously began moving inside. I had no idea how far he wanted me to go, so I just kept moving. As I gazed upward, there was barely a single crack in the thick canopy of leaves. The sentries on their vultures keeping watch from the sky wouldn't be able to see what was going on while we were in here. And that unnerved me.

"Keep going," the sentry called behind me.

Yeah, yeah. Easy to say when your ass is safely back there.

I ventured deeper, my heart quivering at the slightest sound—the crack of a branch beneath my feet, the distant cawing of a bird, the rustling of the leaves… and then, as I looked to my left, I saw something. Something I'd never seen before in my life. The vision was confusing, unnerving and undeniably beautiful all at once. And as the vision began moving toward me, there was nothing I could do to back away. I stood transfixed. Enchanted.

Chapter 17: Hazel

To my surprise, we arrived in a wide-open forested area. I never would have guessed that there was a forest in this place—certainly not one as large as this one. The creepy voices of "dervins" had disappeared by now… apparently they'd completed their job of directing us exactly where they wanted us to go. Tejus paused for a few seconds, his dark eyes spanning the trees, before his hands tightened around my legs and he darted us inside. His strategy in this seemed to be to get through it as fast as possible. But there was only so fast that you could travel in a forest as dense as this. The ground was also terribly uneven, with large bushes sprouting up here and there, causing us to make detours that took up extra valuable seconds.

We hadn't been able to estimate how far the forest stretched—it couldn't have been that far though, for goodness' sake—but before we could even get a quarter of a mile into it, we caught sight of something to our right. Four people. But they were not ordinary people. The man and three women emanated a golden halo and were garbed in clothes of leaves. Their hair was long and their features were perfect, pristine, unearthly. Impossibly beautiful.

"What are they?" I rasped.

"Nymphs," he answered after barely a second's pause.

Nymphs. I had heard only a little about nymphs, but I knew they were supposed to be nature spirits, ethereal beings whom some mistook for marsh dwellers because of their ability to assume a subtle state as well as physical. In addition, they were known for their, *ahem*, promiscuity. Nymphs could hold evil intentions too, I'd heard, but they were not usually evil—they were a peaceful folk… but hardly less dangerous than marsh dwellers in our particular situation.

We couldn't afford to let them enchant us.

"Either do some mind juju fast," I muttered, "or get us—"

Tejus had already launched into a sprint.

The nymphs had already noticed us, however, and they could travel much more swiftly than us. The ground slipped effortlessly away beneath their feet, and soon I felt a tugging on my back. Strong hands grabbed my shoulders and yanked me away from Tejus. It was the man who had grabbed me, the impossibly handsome man. He pulled me back against him, and I found myself pressed against his chiseled chest, while the three women swarmed around Tejus like thirsty bumblebees. He withdrew his sword and lashed out at them, but the blade merely passed through them as they quickly assumed a subtle state.

Nymphs were known for their ability to

manipulate minds; it was how they seduced. I wasn't sure if Tejus alone could hack all of their minds before it was too late… It seemed that the king really had thought through his choice of supernaturals here.

My lips parted as the male nymph twisted me around, firmly yet somehow gently at the same time, and I found myself gazing up into his sky-blue eyes. His lips were full and dangerously kissable, his glossy brown hair perfectly mussed, as though he had just woken from a rest.

"Where do you travel to in such a hurry?" he asked, his voice low and smooth like honey. A voice I could listen to all day…

"I-I…"

His gorgeous lips parted in a smile, revealing white teeth, as he pressed a finger to my lips. His touch sent tingles running through me, turning my insides to mush. This guy… I'd never come across a guy like this before even in a romance novel. I… I wasn't prepared.

"Speak no more," he whispered, "for it matters not. It is too fine a day to not stop in this calm, peaceful forest."

He traced my jaw, which made my lips quiver.

"You must stay a while and rest… You look so tired and hungry… Are you not?"

Even though my conscience screamed at me to deny it, I found myself nodding and my mouth replying, "Yes. I am both things."

"Then come with me … We shall feast and rest."

The sounds of Tejus struggling with the three female nymphs faded out as the male nymph engulfed me in his arms and swept me away into the depths of the forest, carrying me like some kind of prized possession… which I supposed to him I was.

Chapter 18: Hazel

My brain descended into a sickly sweet haze. The male nymph had taken me to the base of a large hollowed-out tree. Within the hollow were soft beds of leaves which served as cushions, and he gathered luscious berries from nearby trees, collecting them within a carved wooden bowl. He set them in front of me and began to feed them to me, one at a time. I couldn't bring myself to wonder whether they were edible for humans, whether they might even be poisonous. I just ate from his fingers while gazing into his entrancing blue eyes.

After he'd finished feeding me all the berries, he

set down the bowl and licked his juice-stained fingers before sweeping a stray strand of hair away from my face and placing a flower behind my ear. Then his eyes roamed my face and settled on my lips, which, to my vague discomfort, I found myself parting, as if beckoning him closer. And closer he did come. He leaned in, nearer and nearer until our noses were touching and then our…

The sound of another man laughing echoed through the forest, disturbing the moment. The nymph drew away from me and gazed outside. I followed his gaze to see another male nymph, just as fine as the one I found myself holed up with, marching within view carrying a familiar blonde-haired girl.

R… R…

As her head turned, I caught sight of her smiling face.

Ruby.

A question pierced my haze. *What is she doing here?* It was followed by a dozen more questions until…

Oh, God. Ruby! Tejus!

I jerked out of the hole like a rocket, stumbling over the ground as I neared Ruby. Her nymph appeared to have already started undressing her. Her shirt was unbuttoned, revealing her bra, and her pants also seemed kind of loose.

"Stop!" I shouted—hoping to attract Tejus' attention, wherever the heck he was— as I leapt toward Ruby's nymph. I managed to grab hold of her right arm and tug at her before my own nymph caught me from behind and pulled me away.

He twisted me to face him, his palms cupping my face.

"What is wrong?" he asked, his eyes drilling down into mine again.

I shut my eyes and attempted to shove him away, but he only gripped my arms, sending more involuntary chills through my body. "Let go of me!"

Ruby's nymph was carrying her further and further away, and it seemed she had not woken up to reality yet.

"But why?" my nymph crooned. "Why are you in such a hurry? We have all the time in…"

A whoosh rushed past me and a split second later, the nymph grasping me went quiet. Opening my eyes to look at him, I gasped to see an arrow shot right through his forehead. His grasp loosening, he teetered before crumpling to the ground.

I looked toward where the arrow had emanated from, expecting to see Tejus standing with his bow. But although it was a tall, dark, long-haired sentry… it wasn't Tejus.

It was Jenus.

He shot another arrow at Ruby's nymph, slaying him too. Ruby went falling to the ground on top of him.

Then, stowing his bow among his other weapons, Jenus loped toward me. Before I could make any kind of serious effort to get away, he'd reached me. Grabbing me with his powerful hands, he flung me high over his shoulder.

Talk about out of the frying pan and into the fire.

Chapter 19: Hazel

No!

Whatever was going through Jenus' mind, it couldn't have been good. That much I could say about him without ever having exchanged a word with him before.

"*What* are you doing?" I seethed. "Ruby is your human!"

"If you remember," he corrected me in a low steady voice even as he continued to lope through the forest, "*you* were my first choice of human."

I suspected the only reason he'd chosen to save me was out of rivalry with his brother. There was no other reason why I should be more valuable in his eyes than Ruby.

"But you can't just carry me off! It's against the rules! I'm Tejus'!" I died a little inside at my last statement. I couldn't believe I was actually yelling that I belonged to that guy, but he was better any day than this monster.

"It's not against the rules to swap—no such rule has been passed. We've reached a communal area—all of our separate paths flowed to here. There's no reason why we might not do a little… mixing and matching in the process."

Ugh. No! This can't happen. What was Ruby going to do now? I was sure that the death of her nymph would snap her out of her daze fast, but she needed to make sure that she wasn't caught again.

And myself… As much as it killed me, I found myself yelling out Tejus' name like a damsel in distress.

But he didn't answer.

I realized why as the sound of three giggling girls came within earshot. As we whipped through the trees, I caught sight of Tejus, backed up against a trunk while the girls, bare from the waist up, fawned over him while twining their fingers in his long hair.

Tejus was no longer fighting them.

In fact, he was butt-naked.

Oh. My. God.

"TEJUS!" I roared.

As his brother carried me right past him, I couldn't stand this any more. I stopped struggling and focused all my efforts on trying to get at an angle to reach one of the sentry's weapons—a dagger. Stretching a hand down, I managed to swipe it. I moved as swiftly as I could, pushing myself into a more upright position before pressing the blade to his throat.

"Let me down," I hissed. "Or I will drive this through your throat."

He stopped still.

"And don't you dare start trying any mind games. I know now what it feels like to have a sentry attempt to enter your mind. I don't care if it will see Tejus disqualified… I'm a woman with nothing to lose."

Apparently he'd underestimated me—thought I was just a weak human girl.

I could practically see the cogs in his brain turning. What options did he have? Attempt to break into my mind anyway, and risk me driving this dagger through his neck?

He didn't know about the deal Tejus had made with me—he didn't know that I couldn't afford to kill him and this was all a bluff.

Slowly, his hands loosened around me. As he lowered me, I was careful to keep the knife pressed close to his body before quickly reaching for his belt and swiping his bow and quiver.

"Now go back to fetch your human," I hissed. "And stick to what is yours in the future."

A mixture of fury and indignation sparked in his eyes, but apparently he wasn't willing to waste his time with me any longer. It would be easier to just fetch Ruby rather than dealing with me battling him at every turn. Thus he turned on his heel and rushed back into the woods. I pitied Ruby being stuck with him, but she needed to get out of this dangerous forest. At least with Jenus she would keep heading toward the center of the maze, where we all needed to head. It would also buy us a little time as Jenus searched for Ruby.

But I had to fetch Tejus first.

I hurtled back toward the sound of giggling. At least I wasn't at risk of falling for those girls' charms. I crept to a tree that gave me a direct view of the four of them standing, and stopped behind it. Peering around the trunk, I couldn't help but roll my eyes.

Tejus might be a master of control… but he was still a guy. Three hot chicks were apparently more than enough to unravel him. I wondered again how Jenus had managed to roam freely when his brother hadn't. Surely there were other nymphs stationed in this forest, waiting?

I shook the thought aside and focused on the task at hand (while I desperately tried to avoid raking my eyes over Tejus' body—he was a finer man than I liked to admit).

Looks like the "damsel" will be the only one doing any saving around here…

As I nocked an arrow to the bowstring, I thanked my grandfather Derek for the archery lessons he'd personally given Benedict, Grace and me. The nymphs were in their physical forms—enjoying contact with Tejus—so if I could just aim right… I shot an arrow against the trunk of the tree they were leaning against, very close to one girl's head. I didn't actually want to kill any of them. Just get them away from him.

I broke out from my hiding place and charged toward them.

"Enough!" I hissed.

They stumbled backward and stared at me, while Tejus' dazed eyes also fixed on me. That was apparently enough to stir him, snap him out of his fantasy land.

Apparently he was mortified, because the first thing he did was leap for his clothes, which were piled in a heap, and pull them on, as I continued to fire arrows at the nymphs. When I reached Tejus, I felt that familiar uncomfortable sensation pass through me. He was regaining mental strength from me, prying himself out of the daze he'd allowed himself to fall into.

Hopefully now he'd get his act together and resist them. They had assumed their subtle states to keep themselves safe from my arrows, though they started to approach Tejus again. He darted toward me and grabbed me before rushing into the trees. Even while he ran, I felt him continuing to drain my energy. The nymphs were still hot on our heels and trying to lure him back into their arms, but he managed to resist. Finally, they gave up and fell back, allowing us to flee.

Recalling something Tejus had told me in a stern voice not so long ago, this seemed an appropriate opportunity to serve it right back to him. Clucking my tongue, I said:

"You must learn to harness your emotions, Tejus Hellswan."

He threw me the deepest scowl.

Chapter 20: Hazel

"I deserve as much of a medal as you do if we get through this," I said sourly, once we'd reached the end of the forest and began to dart back into the maze.

We weren't sure where Jenus was. We hadn't seen him on our way out. Either he was on his way now with Ruby and we had managed to gain some advantage over him, or he had exited the forest and reentered the maze by a different route.

There hadn't been any goblins to inform us of the "moral" of the last obstacle, but I supposed it should be self-evident: brain over passions. Tejus had been caught off guard, and with three goddesses flooding toward him, a small part of him must have allowed himself to be overcome. I couldn't believe that he couldn't have fought them back if every fiber of his being had been against them.

As we turned a corner, a whispery voice above us confirmed my suspicion—the voice of a dervin: "Let nothing, however sweet, divert you from your path."

I groaned internally, fearing that it was going to start following us again and causing us more grief by creating illusions in the maze, but its only job seemed to have been to inform Tejus of the moral, and then we were left to continue alone.

Tejus stopped talking to me. I suspected a large part of that was because he was still embarrassed. But that was okay by me. I was also still recovering… trying to keep my mind off what lay beneath his clothes (which was harder than it should've been since I was clinging to him).

As I thought of my brother, however, I quickly

became distracted. *What's going to happen to him when he and his sentry enter that forest?* For all I know, they could have entered already. But Benedict and Julian were still only kids. I had to hope that the nymphs wouldn't take an interest in them and would instead go straight for Tejus's brothers.

I wondered what could possibly be up next. I felt more nervous than ever as we continued to traverse the maze. Oddly, the temperature felt like it was starting to spike.

"Do you feel that?" I breathed against his ear. "Feels much warmer."

He grunted in acknowledgment.

One of the watchers swooped overhead on his vulture. I waved up at him sarcastically, to which he responded by looking at me with disdain before soaring out of sight.

The further we ran, the higher the temperature climbed until I was positively sweating. I never could handle the heat well, but I didn't have any more layers I could tear off.

Higher and higher the temperature spiked until it grew positively unbearable. The problem was exacerbated due to the fact that I was forced to cling to Tejus. He wasn't exactly the warmest of creatures, but he wasn't a vampire either.

When we reached the next opening in the hedge, we finally discovered what was causing it. Boiling air engulfed us. We were standing about twenty feet away from a moat of churning, molten lava. I was once again left to marvel at King Hellswan's organizational abilities. *How the heck did he pull this off?*

Beyond the moat was an island that was bordered entirely by a high, stone building. Built into its walls, opposite us, were five large doors, each painted with a red cross. Flaming torches were dug into the ground on either side of each entrance. It was obvious that the brothers were supposed to reach these doors.

But how?

We circled the moat of lava entirely, but there was

no bridge. Returning to face the five doors, we did spot piles of heavy rocks.

"We're supposed to build our own bridge?" I murmured.

"Yes," Tejus said tightly, as we approached the rocks. What bothered me was their lack of thickness. Either the lava was not deep or we were expected to pile them to stand on top of one another.

"God, this is madness," I whispered, clutching my forehead. My headache was beginning to return.

Tejus merely swallowed and gathered three large rocks in his arms. I slid off his back to free him up, otherwise the rocks were going to crush my legs. He lost no time in approaching the edge of the lava where he placed the rocks. Then, kneeling on the bank, he cautiously and steadily eased the first stone into the fiery liquid.

My first guess had been correct: this lava was not as deep as it looked. The stone sat fairly easily, its top remaining dry.

Now it seemed to be simply a matter of

replication. Tejus picked up the next stone and, daring to stand on the first, he placed the second in the same manner. As he returned for the third, we were met with a most unwelcome sight.

Jenus emerged from one of the openings in the hedge. He had Ruby slung unceremoniously over one shoulder. His eyes quickly found us. He glared before scoping out the area and spotting his own pile of rocks nearby.

He was able to take advantage of our groundwork, assuming that we had already figured out that the only way across was to build a bridge, and began replicating our actions. After dumping Ruby on the ground, he rushed over and began to collect stones, while Tejus sped up.

"Come on," I said beneath my breath as Tejus placed another stone.

I wanted to help him carry more stones to make things quicker, but they were far too heavy for me to handle. I'd damage my back.

As Jenus began to work with frenzied speed, I

exchanged a nervous glance with Ruby. Poor Ruby. She must have been with her nymph quite a bit longer than I had with mine when I'd found her.

"Are you okay?" I mouthed.

"Yeah," she mouthed back, though she looked anything but. She looked shaken, and like she needed nothing more than a good hug. I wished that I could rush over to her, but it was not a good idea to get so close to Jenus after I'd threatened him in the forest. He might also think that we were fraternizing.

There wasn't a lot Ruby could do to slow Jenus down as he worked. Tejus was still ahead of him, but not by much.

Where is my brother?

Where is Julian?

Almost as soon as the thought entered my head, Julian came into view, emerging from another hole in the hedge with Tejus' other brother, whose name I hadn't even caught yet.

Julian's clothes were ripped, his hair a matted

mess. His sentry hardly looked in any better a state. God knew what they had been through back there. I didn't want to think.

I glanced up at the sky, searching for watchers, hoping to yell out and ask if they had seen my brother, but I couldn't spot them now. *Where are they just when I need them?*

"Hazel," Tejus hissed to me from about halfway across the river of fire. "Come to me now. I can jump the rest."

Oh, gosh. My eyes widened into saucers as I took in the terrifying mass of seething liquid.

But there wasn't time to think. I slanted a quick glance at Jenus—he had seen his brother's idea and he had only a few stones left before he would be in a position to do the exact same thing.

I rushed to the edge of the moat and, spreading out my arms to balance myself, took a leap of faith onto the first stone. It wobbled slightly, which almost gave me a heart attack. One slip, and I was dead.

"Come on! Faster!" Tejus demanded.

Shut up! I felt like snapping back. I was under enough pressure as it was in this moment without him stressing me out.

I took the next step, and then the next… Then I realized that he had started spacing them further apart in order to save time. When I landed on the fourth, I almost slipped, and the gap between the fourth and the fifth was even wider.

Deep breath. I can do this.

Fixing my eyes firmly on the rock in tunnel vision, I leapt again, and then again, until I was one stone away from Tejus. He spread out his legs as wide as he could on the stone before outstretching his arms, his dark eyes willing me to take the final jump.

It took every ounce of courage and blind faith to place my complete trust in this man as I thrust myself forward over the final stretch of lava. There was not enough space on his stone for me to land on my feet. If he didn't manage to catch me, I would sink. But he did catch me. He caught me firmly, one arm wrapping tightly around my waist while pulling me close against him. Then, raising me over one of his broad shoulders in a fireman's lift, he twisted around on the rock and set his focus on the opposite bank. I was both relieved and terrified that I could not see the final jump that he made. It came with a harrowing jolt to my stomach, and I felt like I was going to throw up as we flew through the air and landed with a thump on solid ground. My heart was palpitating like a rabbit's.

Okay. We did it. We did it.

As I glanced across the river back at Jenus, he was about to do the same with Ruby. And very soon after, his third brother along with Julian.

The screeching of vultures sounded overhead, distracting me. The watchers had returned and, to my shock, so had the king. I wondered what had called him here. Maybe this next task had some special significance he wanted to witness?

Tejus glanced up, urgency intensifying in his irises on spotting his father, before he pulled me toward the stone building. I didn't get the chance to yell up about my brother.

We arrived outside one of the cross-marked doors, where he set me down and snatched up a burning torch. Then, with one mighty thrust of his leg against the door, he forced it open. We spilled inside, emerging in a pitch-black hall filled with cobwebs and old, smashed-up furniture. The only light we had was that coming from outside, and from the torch Tejus gripped in one hand. There wasn't a single window. As he cast about the flames, scoping out the room, I realized that it was shaped like a donut. It ended about fifteen feet in front of us, which meant that something else lay beyond that—either it led to another circular room that took up the middle of the building, or perhaps there was an internal courtyard of sorts…

I jumped as another door opened. Jenus and Ruby.

They followed us as we raced to the opposite wall, but there were no doors or windows anywhere to be seen. We followed the wall right around but found no way through it.

"What the hell?" Jenus cursed.

Tejus was breathing hard, his jaw tight.

It suddenly occurred to me how cool this place was compared to outside. Yes, it was closed off and there weren't windows... but stone absorbed heat.

Then Ruby screamed a word which turned my veins to ice.

"Ghouls!"

Her panicked announcement was quickly met by a round of eardrum-bursting shrieks. The flickering torchlight illuminated ten ghouls manifesting from the shadows and zooming toward us, their long bony, clawed fingers outstretched. They were hideous in appearance: long bony bodies, mostly bald skulls, and sharklike teeth.

Not the type of thing you wanted to see coming at you in the dark.

I knew what ghouls did to humans, and maybe even to sentries, who weren't all that different in terms of basic physicality. When they were in their physical forms, ghouls ripped people apart from the inside and consumed their innards. They were also mind-manipulators—hallucination-seeders and deception-instillers. We'd once had a ghoul problem in The Shade, long before I was born, which had caused Mona to believe that Kiev was cheating on her with my grandma Sofia. And then, of course, I'd heard all of my great-uncle Lucas' stories about his time spent in The Underworld, as well as my uncle Benjamin's.

Tejus and Jenus whipped out weapons, brandishing them in front of us. The ghouls, being in their physical forms since they were preparing to maul us, were forced backward a few feet.

Ruby and I would make easy targets and it seemed that the ghouls had already realized this. Their beady eyes fixed on us.

Still holding the torch in one hand, Tejus lashed out with a sword as two attempted to leap for me at once. Practically choking on my tongue, I tightened my hold on Tejus in a panic, though, of course, he needed to be free to fight them off. My eyes passed over Tejus' weapons. I grabbed his spear and held it out in front of us too in an attempt to assist. We backed up into one corner, trying to gain a scope on our problem.

"We have to dismember them," I gasped as they came at us again.

"I know," Tejus said through gritted teeth.

It made me furious to see that Jenus had dropped his torch and was taking advantage of both hands to defend himself—he was relying on Tejus holding a torch. I reached to grab the torch from Tejus—he would be of better use holding two weapons.

He lashed out and managed to catch one of the ghouls in the neck, slicing right through it, while I stabbed one in the gut (which did little more than aggravate it).

The others were fast closing in on us, and as Julian arrived with the third brother, the ghouls went into a frenzy. A third batch of warm intestines to tantalize them.

"Watch out, Ferros!" Julian's panicked voice echoed through the hall.

I turned just in time to see a ghoul wham into the side of Tejus' third brother. It knocked him to the ground, sending Julian flying across the floor. It instantly pounced on Ferros and the next thing I knew, its claws were driving deep into his gut.

"No!" I screamed.

I had lost my mind to panic, not for Ferros, but for Julian. It was going to pounce on Julian next. I was sure that a human would be a more delicious—as well as rarer—delicacy than a sentry.

"HEY!" I bellowed at the ghoul, before hurling my sword in its direction. It made contact with its back—enough to agitate it and make it turn in my direction.

I wasn't prepared for that.

As it came rushing toward me, I went scrambling back toward Tejus... only to be cut off by another ghoul. I ducked and threw myself across the floor, attempting to avoid it, but one caught hold of my right foot. Its bony fingers winding around my ankle, its claws digging into my flesh.

As I felt myself being pulled back, sliding across the floor, I was expecting another hand to grab me higher up my body and rip into my guts.

But something sliced the air and crashed down hard against the stone floor. There came a screech and as I looked down, I realized that the ghoul's arm had been severed.

A strong hand closed around my upper right arm and hauled me up. Tejus loomed over me, his sword dripping with blood. He pulled me against him, indicating that I climb onto his back, before he whirled around and continued to fend off the ghouls.

I was relieved to see that Ruby had climbed onto Jenus' back, while Julian was huddled in one corner, the rest of the ghouls temporarily occupied by the sentries' weapons.

For the first time, I was witnessing Tejus and Jenus working together as they slashed through the ghouls. I could appreciate Tejus' sword-fighting abilities over his brother's. The fact that he could make something as gruesome and bloody as slaughter look almost beautiful said a lot about his skill. There was a smoothness to his movements that Jenus did not possess—a rhythm that came almost like a dance.

Tejus and Jenus chopped and sliced and ducked until they had managed to dismember all of the ghouls. Then they raced with Ruby and me around the room to verify that none were left hiding. Unless any ghouls had gone transparent to hide themselves, the brothers had finished them off.

We met up with Julian back where the main battle had taken place. He hurried over to us, standing in between Jenus and Tejus. The sentries gazed at their fallen brother before gathering around his body, but barely any expression crossed their faces. Like when Tejus had heard the news of their other brother's death, it was as if it was merely a fact of life. Business as usual. Especially now they were in the midst of their father's crazy trials.

The ghouls being vanquished, Tejus and Jenus

quickly slipped back into being enemies again. They started to rush back through the doors we'd entered, when a deafening grinding noise sounded behind us. It came from what had previously been a solid brick wall. Now it was parting, drawing aside like a heavy curtain and letting in light. It created a gap of six feet before stopping.

Then the king's voice boomed down from the sky:

"On occasion, you must learn to cooperate with your opponents."

The brothers hurried outside. The king and his two cronies were circling above us in the sky. I wondered if he would feel anything at all when he saw that his third son did not emerge from the building. But my—and all of our—attention was quickly drawn elsewhere. We had emerged in a grassy clearing, in the center of which was a mound. And on top of the mound was… I let out a soft gasp. A sword, dug into the soil. A mighty silver sword with a handle of what looked like black marble. *The* sword.

As soon as the sight registered in the brothers' brains, they zoomed up the mound at what felt like the speed of light. The sudden jolt made me slip and fall onto the grass, and Ruby fell off a few feet in front of me. Julian approached behind us as the three of us stared with bated breath at the two brothers zooming to the top.

It looked like Tejus was definitely in the lead, but as they reached within ten feet, they stopped abruptly. Blades shot up from the soil like magic, as they had done back in the goblin pit. But these blades were about ten times longer, and much thicker—just as razor-sharp.

The brothers looked up to their father in the sky in confusion.

"Father?" Jenus shouted up. "What is going on?"

The king let his son's question hang in the air for several moments before he descended lower with his vulture.

When he spoke again this time, it was in a quieter voice. "Now you must learn to break rules."

With that, his gleaming eyes passed from Jenus to Tejus, before his vulture flapped him back to his cronies' height.

Break rules.

But there was only one rule in this game to begin with... I froze with fear. The king had given permission for his sons to battle each other.

Tejus' and Jenus' eyes shot to each other's, where they fixed resolutely, their stances widening. They selected a sword each from their belt before leaving their other weapons on the ground.

As Tejus held his blade out, his irises glinted with grim determination. They began to circle and scope each other out.

Jenus was the first to take a swipe. He lashed out at his brother's chest, missing by an inch as Tejus dodged. Then Tejus retaliated, forcing his brother to swerve dangerously close to the wall of blades protecting the prized sword. Jenus was forced to loosen his offense in order to slip away from the blades. He backed down the hill, but this only gave his brother a height advantage. Tejus' sword became almost a blur as he fought his brother further down the mound, until Jenus lost his footing and tripped. I was hoping that Tejus would finish the job off quickly, but Jenus managed to rise and fight back in time, forcing Tejus back a couple of steps.

I became too distracted by Ruby to witness what happened next. She started clutching her head and crying out in agony. Then, before I could stop her, she shot to her feet and started running—faster than I'd thought her capable of in her weakened state. She dashed up the mound toward the two fighting brothers.

"Ruby!" Panicked yells ripped from Julian's and my throats. "What are you—"

She wasn't heading directly for the brothers, as I'd first thought. She was rushing toward their spare, discarded weapons. She picked up Jenus' bow and arrow and... aimed it at Tejus.

"NO!"

But she was too quick. Her fingers and hands

worked at astonishing speed, as though she'd worked this bow a thousand times before… And in a way, she had.

Jenus had broken into her mind.

I should have seen it coming. His father had just declared this final bout a no-rules contest, had he not? And now that Tejus had the upper hand, Jenus was desperate.

Before Julian or I could stop Ruby, an arrow flew from her bow. Slamming into her, Julian and I managed to wrestle her to the ground, but it was too late—the arrow had caught the back of Tejus' right shoulder, causing him to let out a deep groan of pain. Blood spilled down his back. He reached his left hand behind him to tear out the arrow, but he was weakened.

My skin prickled with fear as I felt my own mind being touched; a throbbing headache came on. One of the brothers was trying to break into my head—and it was either Jenus or Tejus.

As Ruby continued attempting to break free, I

found myself suddenly all alone in trying to constrain her. Julian had grunted in pain and let go. He scrambled for the pile of weapons and picked up a spear. Even though my head felt like it was beginning to split in half—so much so that I could barely even see anymore through the pain—I was forced to leave Ruby and hurtle toward Julian. As he aimed the spear, it became clear that it was Jenus who had taken control of his mind. His weapon was aimed at Tejus.

My eyes beginning to water, I managed to snatch the spear from Julian's hands. Keenly aware that I had let go of Ruby, whom Jenus could manipulate again at any time, I had not a second to lose. When Julian launched himself at another weapon, I spun the spear around so that its wooden butt was pointed toward Julian before bringing it down against the back of his skull.

I'd been taught in self-defense lessons in The Shade that if you got the right angle, you could knock a person out without much force. I had managed to meet my mark. Guilt surged through me as Julian crumpled to his knees and rolled onto the grass, but I had no choice.

Ruby had already picked up the bow and arrow again. I leapt at her and knocked them from her hands before attempting to wrestle her once again to the ground. She put up an exhausting fight, clawing at me and constantly attempting to stand. My face flushed from weariness, I finally managed to maneuver her so that she was lying face down on her stomach. Grabbing a dagger, I didn't know what else I could do with her other than knock her out as gently as I could with its hilt, like I'd done Julian. They'd only be used as Jenus' pawns. I knocked the back of her head, causing her to go still, before rising and returning my focus to the battle scene.

Tejus, in spite of his injury and increasing loss of blood, still had the upper hand in the fight. He was managing to keep his brother from gaining ground up the hill, maintaining Jenus' awkward position on the slope.

The pain in my head intensified further still. I sensed that both of them were attempting to devour my energy, or crack me, or both at once. *Oh, God. How am I going to survive this?*

I didn't need the pressure from Tejus. I was planning to help him anyway as best as I could.

I can't crack. I can't surrender!

Biting my lip hard, I stooped down for the bow and quiver of arrows I'd knocked from Ruby's hands. Placing an arrow, I aimed… but damn. It was ten times more difficult to steady the arrow now than it had been back in the forest. My head was throbbing and the scene around me looked like it was shaking. The ground beneath my feet felt unsteady, like I was in the midst of a mild earthquake. I couldn't fire an arrow without being absolutely certain I would meet my mark, or it could hit Tejus—the two were so close to each other. I had to settle on a different plan.

Discarding the bow and arrows, I snatched up the spear Julian had been armed with. Staggering, I ran as fast as I could toward the brothers.

"Hey!" I hissed.

Tejus glanced at me in time to see me throwing the spear. He caught its wooden shaft before thrusting it down toward his brother.

This meant Jenus really had to keep his distance now from his brother.

Tejus would have to manage completely on his own now, however. I doubted I could do anymore more to help him. Perhaps by Jenus' design, I was feeling so much pressure in my head that I fell to the ground.

Tejus hurled the spear, which caught his brother's robe and pinned it to the grass, causing Jenus to stumble and fall. Then, closing the final distance, Tejus stamped down hard against Jenus' right hand and confiscated his sword. He quickly snatched the back of his hair and pulled him to sit upright. Then, before Jenus could attempt to wriggle free again, Tejus moved to slice his throat.

"STOP!" the king's voice resounded in the sky like a thunderclap.

Tejus paused, his dark eyes lifting.

"You have proven yourself, Tejus, my son," the king called down. "You may leave your brother alive."

I felt taken aback that the king had interrupted what should have been the natural flow of events. But I supposed I shouldn't have been. It was clear that the king had a particular fondness for Jenus, and just because Jenus had failed to beat Tejus for the opportunity to represent the Hellswan family in the battle for the kingdom, the king did not want Jenus dead like his other sons.

Tejus' lips were pursed as he maintained his hold on his brother. Then, obeying his father, he let go of Jenus and backed away.

Still lying on the grass, I felt too weak to sit up. My brain felt too drained. I knew it wouldn't be long now until I passed out. I managed to hold on just long enough to see the barrier of blades relinquish into the ground, and for Tejus Hellswan, eldest son of the king, to climb to the hill's peak, approach the mighty sword, withdraw it from the soil, and hold it aloft.

Chapter 21: Hazel

I woke up in a spacious bed of velvet cushions and warm feather blankets. As I opened my eyes, the room was familiar—a large oval room whose entire northern wall consisted of wide windows, and whose floors were padded with deep red rugs. I'd caught a glimpse of it from the hallway of Tejus' quarters before. This was his bedroom. *Why am I lying here?*

Pushing away the blankets, I realized I was wearing a garment that was not my own—a silk, deep purple nightgown.

Then I spotted Tejus in one corner, standing in

front of a mirror. He was bare-chested, examining one of his wounds on his upper arm. And leaning against the wall near the mirror was the silver and black sword.

"Wha-What's going on?" I stammered.

I climbed to the edge of the bed and pushed myself off. I approached him from behind.

"Where's my brother? Ruby? Julian?"

"I kept my word," was all he responded, his voice terse.

"What?" I moved to his front so I could look him in the face. "What do you mean? Is my brother okay?"

"They are all 'okay'. Zerus, my brother whom your brother was accompanying, lost himself in the forest with the nymphs. Your brother was left untouched, however. The watchers found him roaming the maze, lost. As for your other two friends, they came to. I sent them all back to the human realm."

My throat constricted. "Wha-What? When?"

As much as I was relieved that Tejus was telling

me they were safe and had all survived the maze, how could he have just packed them off like that?

"Less than an hour ago," he replied stiffly, before turning away from me and stalking to the opposite end of the room to pick up his shirt and pull it on.

"How could you not have woken me?" I rasped.

"Your mind was drained. You were not ready to wake," he replied. "But they came in to visit you before they left."

I clutched at my throat, feeling choked up as I imagined them bending over my bed, my brother probably pressing a kiss against my cheek.

I hadn't been able to say goodbye, and I had no idea when I'd be able to see them again.

I eyed the black sword with a sick feeling in my stomach. After everything I'd been forced to sacrifice for it, I'd never hated an object so much.

I flung myself to the window and looked out. Evening had fallen. The sun was setting, thin clouds of mist descending over the kingdom.

Then I looked once more around Tejus' room

before eyeing my night gown and asking myself again: *Why did I wake up in here?*

"How come you brought me in here?"

"It was convenient; I could keep an eye on your recovery."

My eyes narrowed on him. "I need to go back," I told him, my voice uneven as despondency began to slip into anger. "I helped you reach your stupid sword. You now have a shot at winning the crown and keeping kingship within your horrid, heartless family, as well as being eligible to compete for emperorship of your country—though I have no idea why anyone would want to be emperor of this bleak, hollow land so much. I can guarantee none of this chase for power will bring you happiness—if you're even capable of experiencing such an emotion." I honestly doubted that he, or any of these people, were.

Tejus had frozen at my outburst, his deep-set eyes trained on me. Then, in a voice that was as icy and devoid of emotion as his expression, he said, "I informed you of the situation."

His words came over me like a harsh winter, squashing any fragile hopes I'd dared to seed and grow throughout our journey together that perhaps, out of gratitude or decency, he would change his mind by the end of it and let me return with the others.

"But why?" I pressed, hating that I was practically begging now. "*Why* can't you let me go back? I don't understand—"

"Because I am bleak, hollow and heartless!" he snarled, suddenly allowing his emotions to spiral. "Just like my father and brothers and country that you so despise!"

I stared at him as he brought a fist down against a dressing table. I hadn't been expecting such an outburst from him… or perhaps a better way to describe it would have been honesty.

I wasn't sure how to respond.

He spoke again after a pause. "Despite what you might argue, you are still of use to me." His voice was quieter, his eyes averting. "I still need you, Hazel Achilles, and that is why I am keeping you… I am more selfish than you could imagine."

As I scrutinized his pale face, something about his harsh assessment of himself didn't ring true. He had let my brother and friends go, at least. I doubted Jenus or his father would have bothered to do that. Then again, I would have hated Tejus even more if he'd gone back on his word and kept them, been even less willing to cooperate with whatever else he needed from me. Letting them go was possibly just a cold, calculated business move.

Whatever the case, one thing was clear:

Unless my family found a way to reach me in this impossibly hidden realm, I was going to be a prisoner of this man and his kingdom for a long time to come.

Chapter 22: Ruby

Being forced to leave Hazel in the clutches of Tejus Hellswan was one of the most harrowing moments of my life. Even more harrowing than when Jenus managed to force his way into my mind and almost cause me to murder Tejus—I still felt fragile, racked with nerves from that experience.

Julian and I gazed down at Hazel's unconscious form, stiff-lipped and pale, while Benedict shed silent tears. We just had to remind ourselves that if we didn't leave when the opportunity presented itself to us, Tejus might change his mind and we might all be stuck here, with no hope for any of us ever leaving.

I was still hoping that on our way out of Nevertide I'd be able to catch a glimpse of something that might help us decipher its location, or the location of its gate. That hope was crushed, however, after we'd been ushered out of Tejus' room by a maid and led to the base of the castle. Three guards were waiting for us there, each carrying fabric sacks. Without asking for permission or even warning us, they approached and strapped the bags over our heads, fixing them uncomfortably tight around our necks. We could still breathe, but the world became dark and undecipherable. The sentries gripped us and led us stumbling down the steps to the courtyard beneath. I sensed that we were approaching the cage of vultures. I heard the clinking of metal, and then the drawing open of the cage door, followed by squawking and the shuffling of wings.

Riding on these giant vultures with my eyes open had been terrifying enough. I was positively trembling as I was forced to mount the bird. I gripped hold for dear life on the sentry who seated himself in front of me.

"Hold on tight, guys," I said nervously to Julian and Benedict.

Then we rose with a lurch that sent my stomach plummeting. We soared higher and higher, the cool evening air swirling around us. The vultures picked up speed, circling several times before diverting in a straight line. How I wished I knew which direction we were headed in. I waited for ten minutes before I could bear it no longer. I dared to remove one of my hands from the guard in an attempt to loosen the sack over my head. But I didn't get nearly that far.

"Keep both your hands around my chest," the sentry barked. "I know your games."

I was forced to replace my hands. I comforted myself that at least when we arrived on the other side of the portal, wherever that was, we would know its location. I doubted that the sentries would bother to take us any farther than the portal. Once they dumped us in the human realm I guessed that they would return immediately.

My heart raced faster as we began to descend, much sooner than I had anticipated. We soared lower and lower until we had to be almost at ground level.

"Are we almost there?" I heard Benedict ask.

"Hush," his sentry muttered.

The vultures landed with a shudder. My sentry pulled me off, my feet touched down. Gripping my wrist, he pulled me along what felt like a dusty track.

Given the fact that they'd left their vultures, I could only assume that we had reached the portal already and they were going to drop us through it. I could hardly even bring myself to be worried about where we might land on the other side. We'd figure out a way to get back to our families. After our spell of captivity in Nevertide, *anything* felt surmountable back on Earth.

As the man began to slow our pace, I was preparing myself for the leap.

But then the sound of rapid galloping came

behind us—horse hooves hitting the ground—as well as the sound of creaking wheels. Then the galloping stopped. Hurried footsteps started, drawing closer and closer until... a second man gripped my arm.

"My Lord," my sentry said, "we are on orders from your brother to send these humans back to their realm."

My breath hitched as the seething voice of Jenus Hellswan replied, "My brother is not king yet."

"No!" I rasped, now desperately moving to tear off my sack. I didn't understand what was happening. Had we reached the portal? Or had we only descended at Jenus' beckoning? I tugged at the rope that fastened it beneath my chin before strong hands secured my arms behind my back. I kicked and fought and cried, but it was no use. I was not strong enough. I was dragged away from where I sensed the portal was, toward the horses and cart. A door creaked open and I was thrown onto a hard wooden floor. Julian and Benedict were thrown in straight after me—their sentries must have decided to side with Jenus and escort them—before the door slammed shut. Finally free to remove our sacks, all of us untied them and pulled them off. We were indeed in a small rectangular wagon. We rushed to the door that had closed and banged and kicked against it, but it wouldn't budge.

Then the carriage began to move again, the horses continuing on their way, bumping us over the uneven road.

I ran to the opposite end, toward where the driver's seat must be. I banged hard against the wall so hard that my knuckles ached.

"WHAT ARE YOU DOING?" I screamed.

A small sliver of evening light suddenly appeared near the roof. A small shutter had slid open sideways, just high and wide enough to reveal a pair of dark eyes.

Then came Jenus's voice again:

"I am not finished with you humans yet."

Chapter 23: Rose

It was baking hot when we arrived in Crete. While stepping out of the helicopter we'd landed near the archeological site, it was like a tidal wave of dry heat crashing over us, with barely any breeze to counteract it. Not the best climate for a vampire.

Caleb and I broke out in a sweat as we debarked from the aircraft. I had been holding his hand, but was forced to let go because of the discomfort. Ibrahim settled a spell of shadow over us as we all gathered outside. We gazed around the dusty, rocky landscape. One of GASP's agents was here to greet us—Mr. Tulios, a tall light blond-haired man with deep tan skin. He shook my parents' hands before inviting us to go on a tour with him of the area so he could show us all the recently observed peculiarities.

He took us first to a small, cordoned-off lane which was lined with five trucks. Their roofs had been systematically dented deep in the center, as though some very heavy weight had trodden atop them. Next, he took us to a dirt track where a large hoof print had been embedded in the sand—larger than a horse's or any other animal one might find roaming naturally around here. Clearly this was what was fueling speculations among the locals that there was a minotaur on the rampage. GASP's team in Greece had already spent countless hours on site, trying to get to the bottom of the mystery, but nothing had come to light yet.

After Mr. Tulios gave us detailed profiles of the humans who had gone missing around the area, he departed and left us to begin our own investigations.

The first thing we did was gather around and discuss.

"I guess to address the elephant in the room first," my father said, clearing his throat as he eyed a Polaroid of the hoof print dubiously, "do we completely rule out a minotaur?"

Most of us looked to the witches present among us. They were typically more knowledgeable about the existence of other supernatural creatures than the rest of us.

"Well," Corrine said, loosening the collar of her shirt while wiping her brow with a tissue, "my belief has always been that the Minotaur is human-concocted mythology. There has never been any actual evidence that it existed… until this, supposedly." She pointed to the Polaroid. "Assuming for a moment that it does exist—and leaving aside questions such as how and from where in the supernatural realm it could originate—why would evidence come to light only now? Why would it only suddenly start being active, after centuries of being believed in? More likely, I suspect, we have some other supernatural on our hands who is using the Minotaur as a cover to fool the locals and go undetected by us."

That definitely made a lot more sense in my eyes. Supernaturals had to tread much more warily these days on Earth with our worldwide organization on the watch. Something—or maybe a group of creatures—who were aware of the general mythology of this area could be using it as a front and... creating artificial hoof prints in the ground? *Hm.*

This proposal was also strange. And I wondered what kind of supernatural would have the slyness and wherewithal to pull something like this off—and what the point was of going to the effort in the first place.

"Well," my brother Ben spoke up, "whatever the case, I guess that our first step is to set up camp and keep watch. Try to spot or gain some sort of clue as to what is frequenting this place."

"Agreed," my father said. "I suggest that we camp

outside the helicopter tonight—scatter ourselves in tents about the site—in order to spread ourselves out and cover as much area as possible."

Nobody had any objections, though I could tell from people's expressions that there weren't many who were looking forward to spending the night in a warm tent as opposed to our comfortable bunks within the chopper.

We spent the rest of the day roaming the place, looking for any more clues that could possibly help us, as well as scouring the area for a hidden gate. We didn't uncover much except for a couple more hoof prints that we found on a road leading to the nearest village. It did seem that the hoof prints were placed deliberately where humans were more likely to frequent and see them. And the fact that there were only the random one or two in any one space was also inconsistent—if this really was a Minotaur, or indeed some other kind of hoofed supernatural in the guise of one, there would have been a trail of prints leading in whatever direction it was heading. Not just two or three scattered randomly on the ground in any one location.

By the end of the day, we were all ready to unwind with some chilled drinks. Vampires might not be able to eat food without feeling sick, but we could consume beverages other than blood—not for nutrition (our bodies could only gain actual sustenance from blood) but to help ourselves feel cooler.

Caleb and I dropped down next to Ben and River among the cluster of rocks where we'd all settled for a rest before it was time to set up our tents, while Shayla came around serving iced tea. We sipped from our straws and stared out at the dimming horizon, while listening to the conversations and speculations going on around us. Mona even suspected that we could have centaurs on our hands. *Centaurs.* That was yet another species of supernatural I had absolutely no experience with or clue about.

"Let's see if things are clearer by the morning," my mother muttered.

Ibrahim lit a bonfire in the center of our circle while everyone who could consume dinner did. Then we returned to the chopper to gather our camping equipment and set up—something that didn't take long. The tents we had (as well as being camouflage-colored) were pop-up tents, which were quick and pain-free to put up and take down. They were also extremely thin, which meant that by the time we had all settled down for the night—although we'd set up at fair distances from each other to cover as much ground as possible—we could hear what everyone was saying or doing as clear as a bell. Most noticeable were Kiev and Mona having some kind of minor tiff… as well as some noises I'd rather not hear coming from Claudia and Yuri's direction.

I groaned, turning over on Caleb's and my mattress while stuffing earplugs into my ears.

"Congratulations for remembering." Caleb chuckled, his voice sounding more muffled to me as he stuffed his own plugs into his ears. Usually I always forgot to bring ear plugs when we went traveling and ended up leeching off of his stash.

I faced my husband and grinned. "I remembered because I was packing some in Hazel's bag just before we left." I paused, thinking of our children. This summer trip was the first one they'd ever been on. Of course, for most of their lives, time away from The Shade was simply too dangerous with all the Bloodless and mass infestation of other supernaturals. But as soon as we felt that the risk was tolerable, we'd wanted them to experience some time away from our island, experience what it was like to mix with "normal" kids. Ashley and Landis and Claudia and Yuri had wanted the same for their son and daughter too. This was exactly what my parents had wanted for Ben and me, too.

"I miss them," I said.

"We'll be seeing them again before you know it," Caleb said, rubbing my back. "I guess that with all of us on the job, it won't take us long to get to the bottom of this Greek mystery. And then we'll be back in The Shade. The rest of the two weeks will pass in no time."

"Yeah," I mumbled, snuggling closer to him. "I know… and then I'll be booking their next trip."

Caleb smiled wryly.

I relaxed in his arms—it was cooler now, at least—and let my earplugs do their job.

As I drifted off to sleep that night, it was to the pleasant dream of Benedict and Hazel frolicking about on a sunny, windswept hilltop, plucking grass and gathering daisies… all safe and tucked away on their little Scottish island.

Ready for the next part of the Novak clan's story?

ASOV 34: A Sword of Chance releases October 20th, 2016!

Pre-order your copy now and have it delivered automatically on release day.

Visit: www.bellaforrest.net for details.

Here's a preview of the gorgeous cover:

Thank you for reading.
I will see you again very soon!

Love,
Bella xxx

P.S. Join my VIP email list and I'll send you a personal reminder as soon as I have a new book out. Visit here to sign up: www.forrestbooks.com

(You'll also be the first to receive news about movies/TV show as well as other exciting projects that may be coming up!)

P.P.S. Follow The Shade on Instagram and check out some of the beautiful graphics: @ashadeofvampire

You can also come say hi on Facebook: www.facebook.com/AShadeOfVampire
And Twitter: @ashadeofvampire

Made in the USA
Monee, IL
08 June 2020